W9-CDM-727

The Ocean Inside

*Youth Who Are Deaf
and Hard of Hearing*

A House Between Homes
Youth in the Foster Care System

A Different Way of Seeing
Youth with Visual Impairments and Blindness

The Ocean Inside
Youth Who Are Deaf and Hard of Hearing

My Name Is Not Slow
Youth with Mental Retardation

Chained
Youth with Chronic Illness

Runaway Train
Youth with Emotional Disturbance

Stuck on Fast Forward
Youth with Attention-Deficit/Hyperactivity Disorder

Why Can't I Learn Like Everyone Else?
Youth with Learning Disabilities

Finding My Voice
Youth with Speech Impairment

Somebody Hear Me Crying
Youth in Protective Services

Guaranteed Rights
The Legislation That Protects Youth with Special Needs

The Journey Toward Recovery
Youth with Brain Injury

Breaking Down Barriers
Youth with Physical Challenges

On the Edge of Disaster
Youth in the Juvenile Court System

The Hidden Child
Youth with Autism

The Ocean Inside

Youth Who Are Deaf and Hard of Hearing

BY AUTUMN LIBAL

MASON CREST PUBLISHERS

Special thanks to the Rochester School for the Deaf for their generous help with this book's illustrations. Harding House Publishing Service is deeply grateful to Scott R. Smith, MD, MPH, a deaf person himself as well as a pediatrician who works with deaf and hard-of-hearing children, for his insights and help.

Mason Crest Publishers Inc.
370 Reed Road, Broomall, Pennsylvania 19008
(866) MCP-BOOK (toll free)
www.masoncrest.com

First edition, 2004
13 12 11 10 09 08 07 06 05   10 9 8 7 6 5 4 3 2

Library of Congress Cataloging-in-Publication Data
Libal, Autumn.
The ocean inside: children who are deaf and hard of hearing / Autumn Libal.
p. cm.—(Youth with special needs)
Summary: The personal story of a boy born with profound hearing loss is accompanied by information about topics related to deafness. Includes bibliographical references and index.
1. Deaf children—Juvenile literature. [1. Deaf. 2. People with physical disabilities.] I. Title. II. Series.
HV2392.L5 2004
362.4'2'083—dc22.   2003018434.

ISBN 1-59084-729-6
1-59084-727-X (series)

Design by Harding House Publishing Service.
Composition by Bytheway Publishing Services, Inc., Binghamton, New York.
Cover art by Keith Rosko.
Cover design by Benjamin Stewart.
Produced by Harding House Publishing Service, Vestal, New York.
Printed in the Hashemite Kingdom of Jordan.

Picture credits: Benjamin Stewart: pp. 65, 74; Clarke School for the Deaf: pp. 113, 117; Comstock: p. 85; Digital Vision: pp. 17, 20; Dover, *Dictionary of American Portraits*: pp. 24, 54, 76, 104 (courtesy of the Library of Congress, Brady-Handy Collection); Life Art: pp. 86, 87, 115; Patricia Therrien: p. 89; Photo Alto: pp. 92, 114; PhotoDisc: pp. 19, 22, 23, 37, 49, 88, 119; Rochester School for the Deaf: pp. 32, 33, 34, 35, 36, 38, 46, 47, 48, 50, 52, 53, 54, 61, 62, 64, 66, 73, 90, 101, 102, 103; The Seeing Eye: p. 78; Susquehanna Service Dogs: p. 77. Individuals in PhotoDisc and Photo Alto images are models, and these images are intended for illustrative purposes only.

CONTENTS

A child with special needs is not defined by his disability.
It is just one part of who he is.

INTRODUCTION

Each child is unique and wonderful. And some children have differences we call special needs. Special needs can mean many things. Sometimes children will learn differently, or hear with an aid, or read with Braille. A young person may have a hard time communicating or paying attention. A child can be born with a special need, or acquire it by an accident or through a health condition. Sometimes a child will be developing in a typical manner and then become delayed in that development. But whatever problems a child may have with her learning, emotions, behavior, or physical body, she is always a person first. She is not defined by her disability; instead, the disability is just one part of who she is.

Inclusion means that young people with and without special needs are together in the same settings. They learn together in school; they play together in their communities; they all have the same opportunities to belong. Children learn so much from each other. A child with a hearing impairment, for example, can teach another child a new way to communicate using sign language. Someone else who has a physical disability affecting his legs can show his friends how to play wheelchair basketball. Children with and without special needs can teach each other how to appreciate and celebrate their differences. They can also help each other discover how people are more alike than they are different. Understanding and appreciating how we all have similar needs helps us learn empathy and sensitivity.

In this series, you will read about young people with special needs from the unique perspectives of children and adolescents who are experiencing the disability firsthand. Of course, not all children with a particular disability are the same as the characters in the stories. But the stories demonstrate at an emotional level how a special need impacts a child, his family, and his friends. The factual material in each chapter will expand your horizons by adding to your knowledge about a particular disability. The series as a whole will help you understand differences better and appreciate how they make us all stronger and better.

—Cindy Croft
Educational Consultant

YOUTH WITH SPECIAL NEEDS provides a unique forum for demystifying a wide variety of childhood medical and developmental disabilities. Written to captivate an adolescent audience, the books bring to life the challenges and triumphs experienced by children with common chronic conditions such as hearing loss, mental retardation, physical differences, and speech difficulties. The topics are addressed frankly through a blend of fiction and fact. Students and teachers alike can move beyond the information provided by accessing the resources offered at the end of each text.

This series is particularly important today as the number of children with special needs is on the rise. Over the last two decades, advances in pediatric medical techniques have allowed children who have chronic illnesses and disabilities to live longer, more functional lives. As a result, these children represent an increasingly visible part of North American population in all aspects of daily life. Students are exposed to peers with special needs in their classrooms, through extracurricular activities, and in the community. Often, young people have misperceptions and unanswered questions about a child's disabilities—and more important, his or her *abilities*. Many times, there is no vehicle for talking about these complex issues in a comfortable manner.

This series provides basic information that will leave readers with a deeper understanding of each condition, along with an awareness of some of the associated emotional impacts on affected children, their families, and their peers. It will also encourage further conversation about these issues. Most important, the series promotes a greater comfort for its readers as they live, play, and work side by side with these individuals who have medical and developmental differences—youth with special needs.

—Dr. Lisa Albers, Dr. Carolyn Bridgemohan, Dr. Laurie Glader
Medical Consultants

Often we look so long at the closed door that we do not see the one which has been opened for us.
—Helen Keller

1

DISCOVERY

Dana sat in the soundproof booth with her baby on her lap. Denzel watched her intently, wide eyes staring from his dark, chubby face. He opened his mouth in a pink, toothless smile, and a bubble welled up between his lips. He lifted a pudgy finger, and the bubble popped at his touch. Squirming with surprised delight, Denzel tugged at his mother's shirt with his moist hand.

Dana smiled and felt momentarily reassured that this was an unnecessary test. Looking at her little boy filled her with joy and wonder. He was so small and so perfect, always watching with curious eyes, grabbing with his little fingers, wriggling and squirming his plump body, anxious to explore. There couldn't possibly be something wrong with her little boy. Denzel was beautiful, healthy, and flawless.

But somewhere deep in Dana's being, gnawing at the walls of her stomach and aching behind her heart, another part of her wasn't so confident. She thought about what had happened just the other day.

Dana had lowered Denzel into his playpen in the living room and turned on the television. The colorful Teletubbies danced across the television screen as Dana headed to the kitchen. She could hear the soft sounds of the Teletubbies laughing and singing as she began to clean.

Unloading the dishwasher, Dana balanced three glasses on the stack of plates cradled in her arm. As she spun toward the cabinet, the wet dishes slipped from her grasp, smashing against the floor tiles in a chorus of crashing ceramic and breaking glass. As the remains of the shattered dishes rang around her, Dana froze, held her breath, and waited for Denzel's frightened wails to begin. But nothing happened. The clatter of the broken dinnerware faded away until there was quiet. The longer she stood in the sudden silence, the more her alarm grew. Why wasn't he crying? Had something happened to him while she was in the other room? The Teletubbies continued to gurgle and coo, but Denzel didn't make a peep. Sure that something must be wrong, Dana rushed across the kitchen floor, heedless of the broken glass that clung to her socks, and ran to Denzel's playpen in the living room. There he was, sleeping peacefully, teddy bear grasped in his outstretched hand, unaware of anything amiss. As Dana turned the television off, a small ribbon of fear wrapped itself about the back of her mind.

At the hospital's **audiological** center, with Denzel on her lap in the small room, Dana reflected on this and other times when Denzel seemed unfazed by loud noises around him. As much as her brain tried to deny it, her heart knew that this test had to be done. She looked at the reflective window in front of her. She could not see through the dark, mirror-like glass, but she knew there was a technician sitting on the other side observing Denzel's every move. The technician's voice came over the room's speakers.

"Ok, Dana, if you're ready, we'll get started. As the tones begin, I'll be watching Denzel carefully for his reactions to the sounds."

Dana nodded and took a deep breath. An array of sounds began to flow from the speakers. They were quiet at first, soft whistles and bumps that even Dana found difficult to hear. Denzel did not seem to notice these sounds, but Dana kept her worries at bay by telling herself that the sounds were gentle and easy to ignore. Soon, however, the sounds became louder. Nevertheless, Denzel's eyes did not stray from Dana's face. As the noises grew progressively more urgent and bothersome, Dana's heart began to race. The technician had warned her that some of the sounds might be loud, but had assured her that they'd only become as loud as Denzel could tolerate. Now, however, the sounds were booming. Surely this was too loud for a little baby's ears. Yet Denzel seemed totally oblivious to the noises that made his mother's eardrums rattle and hum. Dana instinctively hugged Denzel closer to her chest, wanting to protect him from the noises and wanting to protect herself from the truth. Tears slid from her eyes, down her cheeks, and onto Denzel's face. Denzel reached curiously for the tears as they fell and smiled as the warm droplets splashed his skin. As the sounds exploded like bombs around her, Dana knew the truth. Her little boy was deaf.

Released from the suffocating room with its war zone of sounds, Dana nodded her head dutifully as the technician explained that Denzel would need to take another test called a Brainstem Audio-evoked Response; the technician referred to it as a BAER. The BAER would help them identify the degree and type of hearing loss Denzel was experiencing. The technician explained that this test was good for very young children, since the results did not depend on a child's feedback. A series of clicks would be played in each of Denzel's ears, and carefully placed electrodes would convey signals that would help them determine which of Denzel's hearing pathways worked and which did not.

Afterward, Dana tried to concentrate on the technician's words, but all she could hear was the word "deaf" ringing over and over in her ears. The BAER revealed that Denzel had some hearing—but he was still profoundly deaf. The technician told Dana about books, classes, and doctors, but all she could think about was telling her husband that his son was deaf. How could she tell Roger that Denzel had never heard a single bedtime story that he'd read or his beautiful voice as he sang lullabies? Feeling detached from reality, Dana scheduled appointments for more tests and bundled Denzel up for the trip home.

The bright sun glazed the budding trees with a golden glow, but the freshness in the morning air passed unnoticed over Dana as she strapped Denzel into his car seat. Birds chattered merrily, but Dana paid no attention to their cheerful songs. Normally when traveling in the car, Dana would talk to Denzel about where they were going or the things they were passing. Often she turned on the radio and sang to him as he watched her from the backseat. This time, however, they rode in silence. Dana hardly noticed the cars, lights, and signs they passed. Halfway home, sirens sang out behind her, startling Dana out of her zombie-like state. She caught her breath and pulled onto the shoulder of the road. A police car, ambulance, and fire truck raced past with sirens wailing and lights flashing. Gravel pinged and popped off the car windows as the vehicles sped by. Feeling shaken, Dana eased the car back onto the road. As she glanced in the rearview mirror, the sight of Denzel sleeping soundly in his car seat clutched her heart. She knew that any other child would have woken with a start as the emergency vehicles roared by, but Denzel slept peacefully on.

That night, Roger felt tense and unsure as he watched his son from the doorway of the nursery. Denzel sat in his crib with his back to his father and gazed at the mobile of colorful animals turning lazily just beyond his reach. A classical piano tune that Roger loved danced from the mobile as it spun. When Dana was pregnant, Roger had made tapes of classical music. At night, lying in bed, he would stretch a pair of earphones across Dana's swollen belly and play his favorite music to his unborn son. Sometimes he would rest his face beside Dana's round stomach and sing in his pure tenor voice.

Roger thought about all those nights spent talking and singing to his son. Waves of sorrow and loss pushed through his body and stuck in his throat. *It was all a waste*, he thought but immediately regretted thinking such a horrible thing. "Oh Denzel," he whispered as he stepped toward his son's crib. Denzel turned round and smiled at his father. Roger swallowed his pain and smiled back. Then a flicker of hope lit in his stomach. "Why did you turn around, Denzel?" he asked his smiling son. "How did you know Daddy was here?" Denzel simply grinned his toothless grin, but Roger's excitement was growing. He turned Denzel back toward the wall, reset the mobile, and quietly backed out of the room. When Denzel's attention had once again returned to the dancing animals, Roger walked into the room and called his name. Again Denzel turned to smile at his father as he approached. Roger's heart leapt. The hospital must have made a mistake. Of course his son could hear! Anyone could see that. How else would Denzel have known to turn around when he entered the room?

Delighted and relieved, Roger scooped Denzel from his crib and raced down the hall. "Dana, Dana! There's been a mistake."

"Roger, what's wrong?" Dana rushed to the stairs.

"Someone at the hospital made a mistake. Denzel can hear me."

Lines of pain creased Dana's forehead as she shook her head.

"No, Dana." Roger protested. "Just watch. I can show you." He led Dana into the living room where he set Denzel in his playpen. "Now keep his back to me." Roger left the room while Dana tried to keep Denzel occupied. Then, as Roger walked through the doorway, he called Denzel's name. Denzel's eyes strayed to the wall beside Dana. He turned to give his father a smile. Roger rushed to the playpen and scooped his son up with a laugh. "Good boy, Denzel. You heard your daddy didn't you?" He bounced his son in his hands. "See Dana. Why would he have turned around if he couldn't hear me?"

For a moment, Dana's heart welled with excitement as well. She stepped around the playpen, placed a hand on the back of Roger's neck, and leaned in to give Denzel a kiss. As she dipped her head, she glanced in the direction that Denzel had been facing and her heart immediately sank. Their shadows stood dark and silent against the white wall. "No, Roger," Dana said softly. "He didn't hear you. He saw your shadow on the wall. That's why he turned around when you came in." She felt the muscles in Roger's neck grow taut beneath her hand. He shook her arm away and held Denzel gingerly before him.

"Denzel," he spoke softly to his son, "look at Daddy." But Denzel twisted and gazed at Dana who stood tensely beside him. Denzel smiled at his mother and kicked his legs beneath his father's hands. "Denzel?" he questioned more loudly, but Denzel did not turn his head. Roger thrust his son into his wife's arms and walked toward the door.

"Roger." Dana stepped toward him. Without turning round, Roger raised his hand. "Don't follow me, Dana."

"Roger, please," Dana persisted.

"I said leave me alone!" Roger roared and stormed from the room.

As if he knew what had been said, Denzel pressed his head into his mother's chest. Dana stroked his hair as a lump rose in her throat. She looked down at Denzel as she began to sob.

"You're still my perfect little boy," she whispered between gasps. "You're still my perfect little boy." And then she simply cried, for Denzel could not hear what she had to say.

WHAT IS SOUND?

Sound is a form of energy that travels in waves. These waves are caused by the vibrations of **molecules**. When you set a glass gently on a table, the molecules in the glass and table vibrate slightly. The energy from these vibrations travels through the air to your ear, and you hear a quiet sound. If you slam a book on the table, the molecules in the book and table vibrate violently. Larger waves of sound energy travel through the air, and you hear a loud bang. When a bird sings, it forces air through its vocal cords at different speeds, causing the many different vibrations that you hear as song.

How Do Invisible Waves of Energy
Become Sound in Your Ear?

Your ear has three main parts: the *external ear, middle ear,* and *inner ear.* Your external ear is what you see when you look in the mirror plus the *ear canal.* The external ear catches sound waves and funnels them into the ear canal. You can test this by cupping your hands behind your ears and moving your ears around. Can you hear how the sound changes as you move your external ears?

After sound waves are caught by your external ear, they travel down your ear canal to the middle ear. The middle ear begins with the *eardrum,* a very thin piece of tissue that vibrates when hit by sound waves in the same way that the surface of a drum vibrates when you hit it with your hand. Behind the eardrum are three delicate bones called the *malleus,* the *incus,* and the *stapes.* Sound waves cause the eardrum, malleus, incus, and stapes to vibrate. This **amplifies** the waves, which is necessary because sound energy grows weaker as it travels through the air.

The inner ear consists of the *cochlea* and *auditory nerve.* The cochlea is shaped a little like a snail shell and has three important elements: *fluid,* a thin tissue called the *tectorial membrane,* and *hair cells.* When the vibrations pass from the middle ear to the cochlea, this fluid starts to vibrate, stimulating the tectorial membrane. The tectorial membrane passes the vibrations to the hair cells. The hair cells stimulate the auditory nerve. The auditory nerve carries the message into the brain where it is interpreted and registered as sound.

The path that sound travels from its point of origin to the brain is a very complicated one. Every part of the journey from external ear to internal ear is important, and an injury, **malformation**, or malfunction in any part of the ear could result in a hearing loss.

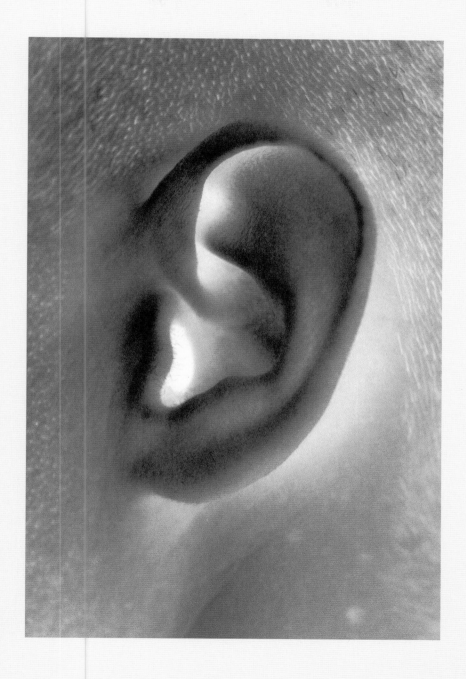

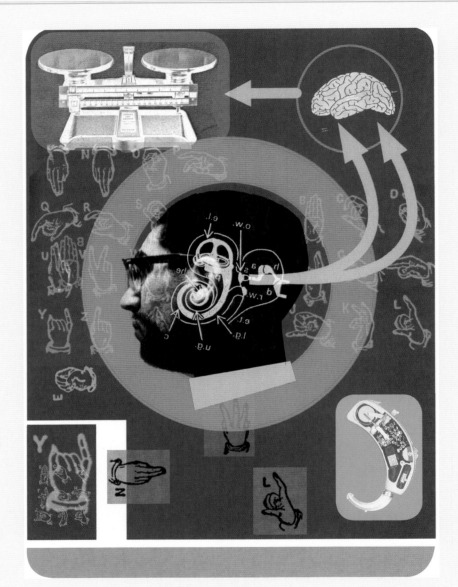

Sound follows a complicated path from our ears to our brains. We use the input from our auditory nerves (as well as from our other sense receptors) to help us decide what actions to take. Hearing aids and sign language are two ways individuals who are deaf may cope with a hearing world.

WHAT DOES IT MEAN TO BE DEAF OR HARD OF HEARING?

Being deaf does not necessarily mean that you cannot hear. Very few people with deafness or hearing loss have no hearing at all. Instead of hearing sounds clearly, however, they may only be able to hear certain sounds, everything might be quieter than it's supposed to be, or the sounds might be muddled. Imagine being in a car with the radio on. The sounds of the music and the voices of the announcers are crisp and loud. Now imagine that your car is traveling a far distance. As you travel, static obscures the music and voices. The signal grows weaker. Everything gets quieter. Perhaps another radio station begins to mix with the one you were listening to. Soon, you can't separate the voices of one station from the music of the other, and everything is muted and filled with static. A person with deafness or hearing loss may experience sounds in a similar way. She might be able to hear something, but not well enough to identify what that "something" is.

There are different degrees of hearing loss. The amount of hearing a deaf or hard-of-hearing person has left is called her *residual hearing*. Whether a person is considered deaf or hard of hearing will depend on how much residual hearing she has. A person who has a large amount of residual hearing would be diagnosed as hard of hearing. A person who has very little residual hearing would be diagnosed as deaf. There are four levels of hearing loss: *mild, moderate, severe,* and *profound*.

How Does a Person Know If She Has a Hearing Loss?

It took months for Denzel's parents to suspect his hearing loss. This is common. Children with hearing loss learn to

A doctor may use an instrument like this to test for hearing ability at various frequencies.

compensate quickly. Denzel, for example, knew when his father entered a room because of the shadow on the wall. When a person enters a room, the child might also react to the vibrations made when the person walks. Because of behaviors like this, it may be months or even years before parents suspect their child has a hearing loss. Once a hearing loss is suspected, there are many different types of tests that can be done.

It can be difficult to test the hearing of young babies because they do not know how to talk and, therefore, can't tell a doctor whether they hear a sound or not. Children under the age of two have their hearing tested using *behavioral observation audiometry* (BOA) and Brainstem Audioevoked Response (BAER).

These are the hearing tests that Denzel received in his

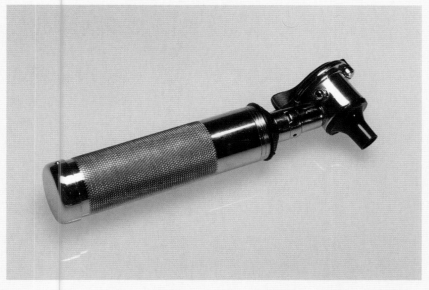

An otoscope allows a doctor to look inside the outer ear at the physical structure within.

visit to the **audiologist**. With BOA testing, a young child either wears earphones or is placed in a soundproof room. Different sounds are then presented, and the audiologist watches for the child's reactions to the sounds. For example, the child's eyes might get wide, he may look around the room to see where a sound is coming from, or he may start crying. The audiologist will also place a vibrating instrument called a *bone conduction vibrator* behind the child's ear and watch for a reaction. Although this type of testing can often determine if a child has a hearing loss, it cannot show exactly what kind of hearing loss or how severe the hearing

Helen Keller did not allow her deafness to keep her from accomplishing great things.

loss is. A BAER test can help the audiologist finetune her diagnosis.

As children get older, other types of tests will be given to determine the degree and type of hearing loss they have.

FAMOUS FACES

Helen Keller (1880–1968)

At eighteen months old, Helen Keller suffered an illness that left her deaf and blind. For the next five years, she was trapped in a dark and silent world. Ann M. Sullivan, a teacher of the deaf and blind, drew Keller out of her isolated world. As an adult, Helen Keller became an author, activist, and even a celebrity. Thousands of people came to hear her speeches and followed the books, articles, and letters that she wrote. Later, a famous Broadway play and movie, *The Miracle Worker*, told the story of her life. Today, people continue to be fascinated by Keller and her amazing accomplishments.

I want to seize fate by the throat.
—Ludwig von Beethoven

2

ALONE

For Dana and Roger, the days and weeks that followed were filled with tests, appointments, classes, and confusion. At night they sat in bed pouring over books about deafness and hearing loss. Often they read through the dark hours and into the early light, trying to find an answer for their one overwhelming question, "How are we supposed to raise a deaf child?" They felt like they were in a race against time. In just a few short months, Denzel would be one year old. The other children his age were speaking their first words, but their son had never even heard a word. The nights of books stretched on, the days of exhaustion grew, and grief began to take its toll.

While Dana campaigned to make Denzel's life as normal as possible, Roger withdrew. He taught music at the elementary school in their neighborhood, and though it filled him with shame, Roger felt a profound sense of relief each morning as he passed over the threshold of his home, stepped outside, and closed the door behind him. As he strolled along the sidewalk, weight seemed to lift from his shoulders. His steps became lighter. For a few brief hours, he could immerse himself in work and forget about the problems at home. But even his work provided only a brief relief from his heartache, for being in the children's presence sparked thoughts about Denzel. The students bounced into Roger's classroom carefree and humming with excited chatter. Roger could not help but look at them and think of how different they were from his silent son. He taught them to play instruments, told them stories about great musicians, and coached them on how to use their voices—all the while thinking how useless the things he had to offer would be to his son.

Soon Roger abandoned the books and articles that flooded the bedroom. He lay on his side next to Dana and pretended to sleep as she studied. Dana knew how much Roger was hurting, but nevertheless she began to feel resentment toward Roger. Each time the resentment sprouted, she tried to cut it back, but its vines were spreading through her, entwining like weeds around her emotions and her thoughts.

She had been working at the local newspaper for three years, and her dream was to be a reporter. She had taken a low-paying job typing the want ads in the hopes of moving up to a higher position, gaining experience, and moving on to a larger newspaper, maybe even magazines or television. But now she looked at her son and knew he needed a parent at home. Logically, she knew their family could not survive on the money from her newspaper job. Roger had to keep working. So Dana put her dreams on hold and quit her job. But still, each day as Roger left the house, Dana felt twinges of envy as she thought about how different her new role as a "stay-at-home mother" was from the professional life of which she had dreamed.

As Dana's time with Denzel increased, she watched Roger's time with his son dwindle. Roger's abandonment of the research they had been doing together was a breaking point for Dana. She studied Roger's back as he pretended to sleep beside her. She felt confused and overwhelmed by how quickly their lives had changed, and she didn't know what to say to her husband. When she finally spoke, bitterness seeped into her voice.

"Don't you think it means something to him? Every night you sat with him and rocked him to sleep. Now you don't go near him at all," she whispered fiercely.

"Why are you whispering?" Roger shot back. He did not turn to look at Dana.

Dana was confused by his question and surprised by the immediate anger in his voice. Her eyes narrowed as she spoke. "Don't try to change the subject, Roger. You don't go near him anymore. Don't you think he knows?"

"Why don't you answer *my* question, Dana?" Roger's voice grew louder. He rolled over in bed to face his wife. "Why are you whispering?" he yelled.

"Shhh, Roger. Don't yell. I'm only . . ."

"Why not?" Roger cut her off, shouting loudly now. "Why not yell, Dana? Are you afraid Denzel will wake up? I'll scream all I want. It's not like he can hear me anyway!" He rolled over and turned his back to Dana.

Frustration and bitterness welled in Dana's throat as she looked at her husband's shoulders. Swallowing her own screams, Dana sank into her side of the bed and turned out the light. Minutes passed as they lay there unmoving, then Dana spoke in a quavering voice into the darkness, "You can turn your back on me if you want, but if you turn your back on him, you don't deserve to be his father." Roger said nothing, but Dana could feel his shoulders begin to shake beside her. She wanted to reach out to him, to comfort him, to hold him the way they held each other before all this had happened. But instead she too rolled onto her side and felt the physical inches between their bodies become an emotional gulf that neither one of them was willing to bridge.

As Roger and Dana lay cradling their individual anger and grief, Denzel sat up in his crib and stared alone into the darkness.

Hours passed. Roger wondered if Dana was asleep. Words of regret and apology rose in him but died unspoken on his lips. Life with Dana and Denzel had always been easy and joyful. He had told Dana he loved her, spoken about his dreams, and sang to Denzel. But now all communication had stopped. How could he tell Denzel he loved him if Denzel couldn't hear? And how could he tell Dana what he was feeling when he was so mixed up inside that he didn't understand his feelings himself? When he married Dana, he had thought he would always be a source of strength for her, someone she could lean on. Now his head rested on a tear-soaked pillow and he felt completely weak and useless. Unable to sleep, he eased out from beneath the covers and crept quietly from the room.

The nightlight shone in Denzel's nursery, illuminating everything with a pale blue glow. Denzel was sitting up, grasping the rails of his crib in his small fists, face pressed against the bars. Roger couldn't help but smile.

"So you're up, too," he whispered to his son. He used to speak to his son so easily, but now he felt self-conscious about his words. Lifting Denzel from his crib, he was shocked at how much heavier Denzel seemed. He thought about what Dana had said. Lately, he hadn't been spending any time with Denzel. Babies grow so fast, changing and getting bigger every day. Roger looked at Denzel and thought about how he had grown and changed in just a few weeks without Roger even noticing. Sitting in the rocking chair by the moonlit window, Roger hugged his little boy. Denzel opened his mouth in a contented yawn and wriggled in the crook of his father's arm.

"I guess I haven't been around that much lately." Roger wasn't sure exactly what to say, but he knew he wanted to talk, so he just said whatever came to mind. "It's not that I don't want to spend time with you, Denzel. It's just that . . . things are so different from what I expected them to be." As Roger spoke, Denzel studied his father's face with curious eyes. He reached for his father's lips and patted his chin and mouth with little hands. Roger sighed. "I know you can't hear me. I want to speak with you so much, but I just don't know how." Denzel's hands strayed to Roger's throat and then danced in the air as he waved his fists.

Roger watched Denzel examine his baby hands and felt overcome with love for his curious little boy. He thought about how a few weeks ago he would have sang to Denzel to tell him how he felt. Roger looked out the window. A crescent moon glowed overhead in the nighttime sky. He looked back to his son and took one of Denzel's tiny hands in his own large palm. He lifted Denzel's hand, pressed it to his throat, and began to sing. His throat vibrated with energy as his voice penetrated the darkness. Roger watched through welling tears as a smile spread from Denzel's lips to his widening eyes. Roger lowered his hand, but Denzel continued to press his little palm to his father's throat. Then Denzel lifted his other hand to feel the vibrations. A glimmer of hope that Roger hadn't felt in a long time began to stir in his chest, and he sang louder.

Standing unseen in the nursery doorway, Dana silently watched her husband and felt hope grow in her as well.

LEARNING TO COPE

Parents often go through a difficult period when they first learn that their child has a hearing loss. They may look at their child differently, or feel that he is suddenly a stranger. Many parents feel much grief and fear as they wonder if the hopes and dreams they had for their child's future will still be able to come true. Furthermore, the financial stress of medical and educational costs can cause upheaval in the household. When it is financially feasible, many mothers (and sometimes fathers) of deaf children will give up their jobs in order to spend more time with their child. The parent may then have a difficult time adjusting to the new role of being at home. This emotional upheaval is normal. However, par-

You cannot tell from looking at these children that they are deaf or hard of hearing. But their inability to hear will require their families to make many adjustments to their daily lives.

Children at the Rochester School for the Deaf enjoy many of the same activities that any hearing child would.

ents must learn to cope with and move beyond their grief in an appropriate manner so that it does not have a damaging effect on their child or on their relationship with each other.

Unfortunately, it is quite common for the parents of deaf and hard-of-hearing children to feel guilty about their children's hearing loss. Parents may wonder if they are somehow to blame, if they did something to cause their children's condition. Parents' feelings of guilt can further complicate the grief process.

We can see that Roger's relationship with Denzel suffers after the diagnosis of hearing loss. Roger no longer knows how to behave with his son, and even though he isn't intentionally trying to hurt Denzel, his behavior has a negative impact on their relationship. Roger and Dana also struggle in their relationship with each other. People deal with grief

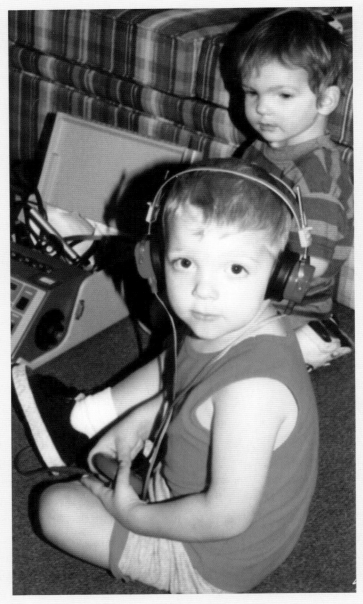

Special schools like the Rochester School for the Deaf offer many services for children who are deaf and hard of hearing.

differently, and Roger and Dana, while struggling to deal with their individual grief, lose their strength as a couple. It is very important that parents who are struggling to accept their child's hearing loss find emotional support so that they can reestablish a positive, supportive, and loving relationship with their child. Doctors, family members, friends, therapists, religious leaders, marriage counselors, support groups, and other deaf children and adults are all people to whom parents can turn for support.

AN EDUCATION IN DEAFNESS

Most hearing people take their sense of hearing for granted and never question what life would be like if they could not hear. Think for a moment how difficult it would be to

This classroom at the Rochester School for the Deaf is far quieter than the typical classroom in a public school.

High school students at the Rochester School for the Deaf enjoy participating in sports.

interact with other people if you could not hear them. How do you think you would learn to speak if you could not hear? How would you learn to read if you had never heard any of the words you were reading? What do you think it would be like to laugh if you couldn't hear laughter? Each year, about four thousand children are born deaf in the United States alone. Furthermore, 10 to 15 percent of all children are born with a hearing loss of some type. And yet, many people never ask themselves what it would be like to have a hearing loss.

Despite the fact that hearing loss is a relatively common thing, most parents, like Dana and Roger, are unprepared for the news that their child has a hearing loss. The time directly after such a diagnosis is often one of great confusion as the parents wonder how they will raise their child and teach their child to communicate.

The first three years of a child's life are the most important ones for language development. In order to speak,

Many people assume that because a child is deaf or hard of hearing he is not as bright as other students. Deafness and intelligence, however, are two separate qualities. Many students who are deaf have sharp intelligence and keen intellectual curiosity.

learn, read, and even think, a person needs to know a language. Most people learn language by hearing the language as it is spoken to them. However, parents with a deaf or hard-of-hearing child face a much greater challenge in teaching language to their child. There are a number of different paths that parents can take in this education process, and many parents enter into a world of exhausting and confusing information and literature trying to determine what method will be the best for their family.

One of the best resources for parents as they struggle to understand their child's hearing loss and what communication method to adopt for their child is speaking with other parents of deaf and hard-of-hearing children—and with other deaf and hard-of-hearing children and adults. These individuals have often learned much from their own experi-

Students at the Rochester School for the Deaf learn without the use of voices.

ences and can give valuable guidance to families who are just beginning their journey into understanding hearing loss.

FAMOUS FACES

Ludwig von Beethoven (1770–1827)

Ludwig von Beethoven is probably one of the most famous deaf people ever to have lived. Beethoven was already a musician when he began to lose his hearing in his late twenties. He went on to create some of his most famous musical works after becoming deaf. Beethoven used the vibrations made by his piano to feel the music he composed. Because of his deafness, Beethoven strove to create music that could actually be felt rather than merely heard. Many people even feel that it was Beethoven's deafness that allowed him to make music that was so haunting and beautiful.

Be courageous! . . . Have faith! Go forward.
—Thomas A. Edison

3

Breaking the Silence

As Denzel grew up, he thought of sound as a mysterious, mind-stretching thing. He could hear a few sounds, but he couldn't figure out what those sounds meant. Half the time, he just ignored what he could hear because none of it made any sense. At other times, however, he would try to imagine what sound must be like for other people. Then he concentrated on sound intensely. He tried to picture sound, to feel sound, to smell and taste sound. Because he could not hear, Denzel tried to imagine sound the way people forced to walk imagine what it might be like to fly. But, no matter how he tried, Denzel could not imagine what this thing called "sound" was supposed to be like or how it would feel to hear the way other people hear.

Sitting with his mother at the kitchen table, Denzel was overwhelmed with frustration. He watched his mother closely and took deep breaths, trying to keep his feelings at bay. Her lips moved in slow, exaggerated formations, but the sounds she made were as muddled as everything else. The harder he tried to understand what she was saying, the more frustrated he felt. Why did they have to do this every single day? No matter how hard he tried, he couldn't understand her, and she couldn't understand him. His mother started the sentence over again. Denzel's frustration quickened and expanded into a rage that made his heart pound. He could feel the emotions clogging his throat and felt powerless to stop them as they forced his mouth open. He couldn't hear the sound of his own

41

voice, but he was completely engrossed in the feeling of his screams as they burst like physical things from his throat.

Tantrums were still a common thing for five-year-old Denzel. Dana and Roger had decided when Denzel was still very young that their little boy was going to learn to listen, speak, and communicate in the hearing world. They had read cases of children with profound hearing losses who, with the help of medical listening devices and intensive education programs, learned to use their residual hearing to understand speech and even learned to speak themselves. They wanted Denzel to function in the world like everyone else, and they were sure that with the best hearing aids, intense speech therapy, and lip-reading they could make it happen.

But Roger and Dana hadn't understood how hard learning to listen and speak was going to be for Denzel. They had expected miracles from Denzel's hearing aids—miracles that never materialized. Denzel hated his hearing aids. The first time they put them in, Denzel became frightened, tore at his ears, and cried for two hours. He didn't understand what the hearing aids were, and the new faraway sounds he heard were baffling and frightening. Dana and Roger hadn't understood the limitations of hearing aids; they could make everything louder, but they couldn't make anything clearer or easier for Denzel to understand. Making things additionally complicated was the fact that the hearing aids even changed and distorted some sounds, so even if Denzel could hear some things through the hearing aid, those things would never sound the way they did to his parents. To top it all off, Denzel was prone to ear infections, so even when his parents could make him wear his hearing aids, he cried from the pressure the aids put on his sore ears.

Despite all of these setbacks, Dana, Roger, and Denzel labored on. Often they felt like giving up, but then something would happen to raise their spirits and give them the strength to press forward.

While Dana watched Denzel's screaming tantrum at the kitchen table, she thought back to one of those happier times. Denzel had been three and a half years old, and school was already a regular part of his life. Twice a week for a year Dana and Denzel made the two-hour trip to a program for deaf children where he was being taught how to listen and to speak. School was a regular part of Dana's life as well, as she took classes on the education of deaf children and practiced Denzel's lessons with him every day.

As a very little baby, Denzel had made many of the same gurgles, coos, and cries that other babies made. But as he got older, he **vocalized** less and less. By the time Dana had her first suspicions that something might be wrong with Denzel's hearing, he hardly made noises at all, with the exception of crying. All her books about babies said that he should be babbling and speaking his first simple words.

When Denzel began attending speech classes, he slowly started using his voice again. But it was nothing like Dana and Roger had hoped. Denzel "spoke" in strange noises that sounded to them like grunts, growls, and moans. Dana and Roger watched their son and felt almost physical pain as he attempted to communicate with unintelligible noises. His little face grew hot and his frustration increased, but they just couldn't understand what he was trying to say. Inevitably, each attempt to communicate dissolved into a mess of Denzel and Dana crying and Roger trying to pick up the pieces. The young parents could not help but wonder if they had made the right choice for their son.

But then one day, they found reason again to hope. Roger had come home from work a little early. He went to the living room where Denzel was pushing a yellow truck across the floor. Not wanting to startle his son, Roger walked in a large arc into Denzel's vision. Denzel's face lit up with surprised delight. He ran to Roger, hitting his father's leg full force and wrapping his arms around his calf. Roger laughed and messed his hand through Denzel's hair. Looking into his father's smiling face, Denzel raised his arms, waved his hands, and demanded simply, "Up." Coming from Denzel's untrained voice, the little word sounded more like "ub," but Roger knew exactly what Denzel meant. Bursting with joy, he scooped his son up into his arms, twirled him in a circle, and ran to tell Dana the news. After that day, more words came like "dad" (which sounded more like "dund") and "mom" (which Denzel pronounced "mmmum"). Dana and Roger knew they had to be patient with Denzel's language development and were seldom bothered by his incorrect pronunciation. Nevertheless, the words came slowly, and now that Denzel was five years old, Dana was all too aware of how easily other children his age spoke with their parents and how much Denzel still struggled to communicate. Now Denzel attended his school four days a week, but she knew he was still far behind other five-year-olds who were already beginning school in regular classrooms and were even learning to read.

Dana sat silently as she watched Denzel's tantrum ebb and flow. Gradually, the shrieking screams waned to gasping cries, then to hiccups. Finally, Denzel laid his tear-streaked face against the table and quietly whimpered. Feeling beaten and fearing that perhaps failure really was at hand, Dana heaved her limp son from his chair, carried him to the living room couch, and rocked him until he fell into an exhausted sleep. When Roger came home, she related the day's events, and he shook his head. Today had been too much like all the days before.

That night after Denzel had been put to bed, Dana and Roger sat down to discuss something new. One of Roger's coworkers had told him about an educational method they had never considered. It was called cued speech. Dana was skeptical at first. When she and Roger had first been given the news that Denzel was deaf, many people had tried to convince them to learn sign language and raise their son this way. Wanting Denzel to have what they thought would be a normal life, they resisted fiercely. As Roger described cued speech, Dana thought it sounded too much like sign language. Seeing her resistance, Roger produced a book his fellow teacher had given to him. "Okay," he began, "before you make up your mind, just look at this." Showing her a diagram in the book, Roger explained, "It's not the same as sign language. There aren't any signs for words. Instead, there are signs for the consonant and vowel sounds. We would still be speaking to Denzel the way we always have, except we would be showing him with our hands what sounds we were making as we spoke. That way, he could still be listening and lip-reading, but if he couldn't hear or see what sound we were making, he could tell by our hands. It would be like making the words we were saying into something visual as we spoke." Dana heard the hope in his voice.

"I just don't know, Roger. We talked about signing before and agreed that if we taught Denzel to sign, then he'd only be able to understand us and other signers. How many people know sign language in this world?" Dana's voice was rising, her anxiety taking over. "He'll grow up totally isolated, only able to talk with a few people and . . ."

"Shhh." Roger cut her off by placing a finger gently on her lips. "I know, Dana," he began quietly. "I know we've discussed this. I'm not trying to upset you." He paused and took a deep breath before continuing. "It's just that every day I go to work and teach children who are not much older than Denzel, and I see how different their lives are. You and I both know that he's being left behind. You know that we've always agreed about sign language, but I really think this is different. . . . But you know, Dana, even if it's not different, I think we have to make a decision here. If we don't do something to help Denzel now, I'm afraid that before we know it, it's going to be too late."

Dana took the book Roger held out to her and began to leaf through its pages. "While you're looking at that, I'll make some coffee. Then we'll sit and talk about this," Roger said. Dana nodded without looking up. By the time Roger returned with the coffee, she'd already made up her mind.

"Let's do it," she said to him as he entered the room. "Let's try cued speech."

TEACHING LANGUAGE TO DEAF AND HARD-OF-HEARING CHILDREN

Dana has given up her job outside of the home and dedicated herself to being not only Denzel's mother but his teacher as well. All parents are both caregivers and teachers, but parents of deaf children need to learn new ways to communicate with their children. This takes time and effort, and it can be hard on both the parents and the children as parents struggle to adjust their expectations of the parent-child relationship.

Parents of deaf and hard-of-hearing children have a number of communication options to choose from when it comes to teaching language to their child. These methods include the *auditory-verbal approach*, the **bilingual-bicultural** approach, *cued speech*, and *total communication*. In

Language acquisition is a major part of the activities in any school or classroom designed specifically for students who are deaf and hard of hearing.

Students at the Rochester School for the Deaf participate in a variety of activities designed to help them cope with their hearing loss.

the past, there has been a great deal of controversy in both medical and deaf communities concerning which approach is the best. This debate may never be fully resolved, but each approach has both positive and negative attributes. Individual families should be encouraged to educate themselves about these communication methods and then decide which is best for their needs. Families should not feel as though they have to do this alone, though. Service providers can offer the resources to help families engage in a thoughtful learning process.

The Auditory-Verbal Approach

The auditory-verbal approach is the first approach to education and communication that Dana and Roger try with Denzel. When most hearing people think of deafness, they think

A classroom teacher uses sign language to communicate with her students.

of people using sign language. However, in the auditory-verbal approach no sign language is used. This approach is an oral method of communication, meaning that children will use their voice, rather than their hands, to speak. In this approach, people who are deaf or hard of hearing use hearing aids or cochlear implants to enhance their residual hearing. (A cochlear implant is a medical device that is surgically implanted to replace a malfunctioning cochlea. You will learn more about cochlear implants and how they work in chapter 7.) Then they learn to use their residual hearing to understand their own and other people's voices. The goal of the auditory-verbal approach is to raise children who are able to speak with hearing people well enough to function fully in the hearing and verbally speaking world.

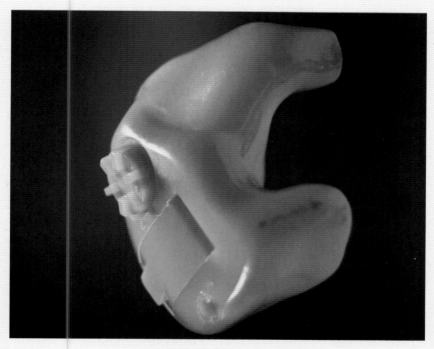

A hearing aid fits inside the outer ear.

*Children who are deaf and hard of hearing enjoying a
Halloween party at the Rochester School for the Deaf.*

With new advances in medical technology, many deaf or hard-of-hearing people who could never have done so before are now able to understand speech. However, no current medical technology can give a deaf or hard-of-hearing person natural hearing. One of the limitations of hearing aids is that they cannot distinguish between sounds; they simply make everything louder. This is not always helpful for a deaf or hard-of-hearing person. Think about how hard it is to understand someone who is speaking to you in a noisy place. This is kind of what it is like for a person with a hearing aid. The hearing aid doesn't just make people's voices louder, it makes *everything* louder and can even distort some sounds, making them even harder to recognize.

Like Denzel, many children have a hard time adjusting to their hearing aids. Even once they adjust, it is always hard work to distinguish voices and what they are saying from all the other sounds. Learning to listen can be exhausting for children. Think how tired you would become if you had to constantly strain to hear everything anybody said. How long do you think you could pay attention before you stopped listening and just let all the sounds blend together again? It takes many years for children using the auditory-verbal approach to master listening and speaking. Some children flourish with this approach, but other children will learn better from other communication styles. When they are young, children who use the auditory-verbal approach usually attend classes and schools that teach them to listen and speak. The child then **integrates** into a school with hearing children. This process of training deaf children to attend hearing schools is called *inclusion*. Inclusion is often the goal of other communication approaches as well.

Cued speech provides another option to teachers of the deaf and hard of hearing.

Cued Speech

Some children have great success with the auditory-verbal approach, but others, like Denzel, struggle with it. Some people don't have enough residual hearing to understand speech and choose to lip-read instead. However, lip-reading is very difficult because many important sounds are made in the throat or in the back of the mouth where they can't be seen. Even a very good lip-reader can only understand about half of everything that is said by watching a person's lips and must guess at the things he cannot understand. Cued speech was developed to help people lip-read more successfully.

Cued speech is a method of communication in which deaf people rely both on lip-reading and on visual cues to understand speech. For example, the words *mat* and *bat* look the same on a person's lips. Someone reading your lips when you spoke these words would not be able to tell which word you had used. Try this exercise. Looking in the mirror, mouth the words "pan," "man," and "ban." Now try "pear," "mare," and "bear." If you had to rely on your vision alone, how would you tell these words apart just by looking at someone's lips? Cued speech makes it easier for people to read lips by giving hand signals to show which sound a person is making. In cued speech, there are eight hand shapes for different consonant sounds and six locations on the face for vowel sounds. If you were using cued speech and saying the word "pan," you would make the "p" hand shape by the "a" location on your face.

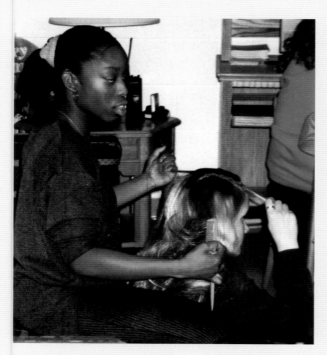

Cued speech would not be possible in a situation where one person is behind the other, as is the case with these two girls who are deaf. Individuals who are deaf need to see the speaker in order to "hear."

Cued speech is different from sign language because the cues are meaningless if used alone. Each hand or face cue stands for a number of different sounds, and a deaf person needs to see what the speaker's lips are doing to determine which sound the cue stands for in that particular situation. Therefore, cuing must always accompany speaking to make sense. Cued speech sounds complicated, but it is actually very simple to learn. Most people only need a few classes to get the hang of cued speech. Children who know cued speech often have **interpreters** in their classrooms who "show" them what the teacher is saying. Children who know cued speech may be able to easily understand their family members, interpreters, and other people who use cued speech, but might still have a hard time lip-reading with people who don't know this communication system.

Thomas Edison, the inventor of the light bulb and the first motion pictures, began going deaf at the age of twelve.

FAMOUS FACES

Thomas Alva Edison (1847–1931)

Most people know Edison for his invention of the telegraph, work on the light bulb, and creation of the first motion pictures. However, few people know that Edison began going deaf at the age of twelve. His hearing loss, however, didn't stop Edison from going on to be one of the most important inventors of the century. In fact, he often told people that his deafness was an asset, allowing him to have plenty of peace and quiet for contemplating inventions and forcing people to put his contracts and agreements into writing.

Prejudice is the child of ignorance.
—William Hazlitt

4

BUMPS IN THE ROAD

Denzel loved walking to school every morning with his father. Walking down the sunlit streets with this tall, confident man who swung his briefcase and whistled merrily made Denzel feel purposeful and important. Denzel still hated his hearing aids, but if he wore them, and if the street was very quiet, and if he listened very hard, he could sometimes pick out the faint tones of his father's whistling among the collage of outdoor noises churning in his ears. When he heard his father's whistles, he felt a great sense of accomplishment and his chest puffed out with pride. Then a car would roar down the street, and the whistles would be lost.

Many things had changed for him since he began cued speech. Two weeks after they had started this new communication method, Denzel felt like something just clicked in his head. Each day, he understood more of what his parents were saying. Understanding more about what words were supposed to sound like was helping him with his own speaking as well. He and his parents worked out a system for practicing sounds and for when they couldn't understand what Denzel was saying. Denzel would show his mom and dad the cue for the sound he was trying to make, and then they would show him the cue for the sound he was actually making. Then Denzel would try again until he made the right sound. When the correct sound finally came out, he concentrated on remembering what it felt like to make the sound so that he could do the same thing in the future. Denzel still had to work just as hard as before to learn to communicate, but the difference now was that he felt like communication was possible. The uncontrollable frustration arose less and less, and after a year, Denzel stopped having tantrums.

Now Denzel was nine years old and was finally able to go to the school where his dad taught music. He liked lots of things about this school. For one thing, he got to walk to work with his dad, and he got to spend all day with Julia. Julia was his interpreter and went to all of Denzel's classes with him. As the classroom teacher spoke, Julia would cue and sometimes repeat what the teacher had said just for him. This was especially important when the teacher did things like turn toward the blackboard or walk someplace where Denzel couldn't see her.

But there were also things that Denzel didn't like about his school. He was nine, but the school made him be in the class with the eight-year-olds because he couldn't read very well. He didn't like his teacher, Ms. Thompson, either. She had lips that were very hard to understand, and she always forgot to turn toward him when she spoke. Denzel got frustrated with lots of the kids in the class as well. Sometimes, when different kids started speaking fast, Denzel could not follow the conversation, and then he got bored. There was one boy in particular who always made Denzel mad. His name was Alex. At recess, Alex would often come to talk to Denzel, and for a minute, Denzel would feel happy and try to speak very clearly and slowly so that Alex could understand what he was saying. But then Alex would turn to the other kids and say something to make them laugh. Often he turned his back or whispered when he did this, and Denzel didn't know what he was saying. Sometimes Julia came out to recess with Denzel. When she did, Denzel would ask her to tell him what Alex had said, but Julia always said it wasn't important and that Denzel shouldn't pay attention to boys like Alex.

Today, class was going particularly badly for Denzel. Julia was sick and hadn't been able to come to school, so Denzel spent the whole morning feeling lost. Ms. Thompson acted exasperated every time Denzel asked her to repeat something. Denzel felt relieved when they began their daily science unit. He was always good at science.

Today Ms. Thompson said she had something special for the class. She asked the children to sit in a circle on the floor. Then she went behind her desk and brought a glass container out for the children to see. Inside the container, a gooey mass floated in some brownish water. Ms. Thompson asked the class, "Who can tell me what these are?" Wanting to impress Ms. Thompson, Denzel waved his hand and Ms. Thompson called his name.

"They're frog eggs," Denzel said, being careful to speak very slowly, trying to pronounce each syllable correctly so Ms. Thompson would understand. "And they will turn into tadpoles, then pollywogs, then frogs." He thought he had spoken very clearly, but Ms. Thompson pursed her lips.

"You're going to have to do better than that if you want me to understand you, Denzel," she replied in an exasperated tone. Accustomed to having to repeat himself, Denzel began again.

"They are frog eggs that turn into tadpoles, then pollywogs, then frogs," he tried again as the children sitting around him began to giggle. He thought he was speaking very clearly, but he knew that sometimes his voice was hard for other people to understand, so he began preparing to try the sentence again. Ms. Thompson, however, wasn't having any patience.

"I can't understand you, Denzel. Someone else," she said shortly, looking around the class. This time Alex waved his hand, and when Ms. Thompson called on him, he stretched his words out in long, exaggerated syllables.

"Those arrre frrrog eggs," he drawled, throwing Denzel a smug smile. "They will be-come tad-poles, then pol-ly-wogs, then fr-rrogs." Ms. Thompson acted like she didn't notice how Alex was mocking Denzel.

"Thank you, Alex." She praised him with a smile. "Now who else can tell me something about frog eggs?"

For the rest of the class, Denzel bit his lip and tried to keep his emotions under control. He felt the sniffles burning in his nose, but he fought them off until recess mercifully came. At recess, he sat alone on a swing. He was trying to swallow the bitterness that the frog egg incident left in his throat when Sandra sat down on the swing next to him. Denzel liked Sandra. She always looked at him when she spoke and often asked him if he understood what she had said. She didn't mind repeating herself and didn't seem bothered by the way Denzel spoke. Sometimes she even explained the things he said to the other kids when they didn't understand. When Denzel first met Sandra, she had told him about how her grandfather lived with her and how he had lost his hearing after flying airplanes in a war. She touched Denzel's shoulder and he turned to look at her.

"I hate that Alex," Sandra said to Denzel. Denzel didn't want Sandra to know that he'd been crying, so he swallowed his hiccups and gave Sandra a reluctant smile. Sandra smiled back. "You want to play basketball?" Denzel nodded his head and followed her to the basket.

Sandra liked sports more than any other girl Denzel knew. By the time recess was over, they were having so much fun that Denzel had forgotten all about what happened with Alex. Feeling sweaty and tired from playing basketball, Denzel plopped down in his chair. A crumpled piece of paper fell from his desk to the floor. Curious, Denzel picked it up and smoothed the crinkles. Printed carefully on the paper were the words, "My dad says you are deaf and dumb."

Denzel looked at the sentence and felt a great confusion and anger stirring in his stomach. Without looking up, he quietly crumpled the paper and shoved it deep into his pocket.

LEARNING TO TALK ALOUD

Think how hard it would be to talk if you could never hear what you were saying! Denzel has learned to speak using his voice, but many people still can't understand him. The voices of people who are deaf or hard of hearing may sound strange to a hearing person. This is because deaf and hard-of-hearing people cannot hear what they are saying, so they don't always know how loudly they are speaking, if they are using proper rhythm, or if their pronunciation is correct.

In speech classes, a deaf child will use many tools to learn how to use her voice. She will place her fingers on her teacher's lips so that she can feel how the teacher's lips move and how fast the air comes out of the teacher's mouth as she speaks. The child will place her hand on her teacher's throat and chest to feel the vibrations that are made when her teacher talks. Then the child will repeat the words with

Cheerleaders at the Rochester School for the Deaf use their bodies to express their enthusiasm.

In the United States, children who are deaf and hard of hearing are legally entitled to a "free and appropriate" education.

her hands on her own lips, throat, and chest, trying to re-create the same patterns, air **expulsion**, and vibrations. When the child pronounces a word correctly, she must remember not how the word sounds but how the word feels when she says it correctly.

AN EQUAL EDUCATION

According to federal laws, schools must provide "free and appropriate" education to children with special needs such as deafness. In some cases, this means providing interpreters like Julia. In other cases, this may mean providing special classes or schools for deaf or hard-of-hearing children.

However, just because a law requires that schools give deaf children an equal education, does not mean that the schools or teachers are always equipped to give a deaf child the education she needs. Many teachers still do not know about the special educational needs of deaf children and find themselves unprepared for the challenges of having a deaf or hard-of-hearing child in their classroom. The fact remains, though, that the law protects the rights of children like these. Parents or other advocates can insist that children receive the "free and appropriate" education the law guarantees each student with special needs.

THE PROBLEM WITH BOREDOM

Denzel sometimes gets bored in his class. Boredom is a common problem for any child who cannot understand or communicate easily. Hearing people need to make an additional effort to make sure a deaf person is being included in a conversation. When the people around a deaf child get involved in a conversation that the deaf child can't follow, the result is that the child will often get bored or "tune out." If you are having a conversation with a deaf or hard-of-hearing person, you should remember to face him and keep your hands away from your mouth so that he can see what you are saying.

DISCRIMINATION COMES IN MANY FORMS

Denzel is only nine years old, but he's already experienced discrimination. Deaf children often face discrimination in the classroom and struggle with teachers and children who do not understand deafness. In the past, deaf people were often called "deaf and dumb." People assumed that just because a person was deaf, or because his voice sounded different, he must have mental disabilities. This of course is not true, but many people today still discriminate against deaf

Children who are deaf enjoy "playing house," just like other children their age.

Signs like this one protect children who are deaf or hard of hearing.

people, assume that deaf people cannot speak, and assume that deaf people have mental disabilities.

Discrimination because of their hearing status is not the only prejudice faced by children with hearing loss. Racism continues to be a far too common thing in our society, and depending on their racial or **cultural** background, deaf children can struggle with multiple forms of discrimination. Denzel is struggling with a teacher who does not fully understand his needs and appears to discriminate against him in the classroom. When situations like this one arise in the future, it may be difficult for Denzel to determine whether he is encountering discrimination because he is deaf or because he is black. In either case, it is the school's job to correct the situation.

Every child comes from a unique familial, social, and cultural background. Educators sometimes become so focused

Because our world is far from perfect, the members of this team of deaf and hard-of-hearing students may face discrimination outside their school.

on the fact that a child is deaf that they forget other important parts of the child's identity. All children face challenges as they grow, and it is important that educators and families see deaf children as whole children with the same educational, social, and cultural needs and challenges that other children require.

FAMOUS FACES

Tilly Edinger (1897–1967)

Tilly Edinger became deaf when she was a teenager, but that did not stop her from becoming a paleoneurologist (a person who studies fossilized brains)! In fact, Tilly Edinger founded the field of paleoneurology. Edinger was born in Germany. During the Nazi occupation, Edinger performed her scientific work in secret for as long as possible. As the Holocaust raged on, Edinger escaped to America. Her brother, however, died in a concentration camp. After the war, Edinger made trips back to Germany to help rebuild paleontology and the scientific community there. In her life, she defied racism, sexism, and discrimination to achieve her goals and redefine science in her time.

Pick battles big enough to matter, small enough to win.
—Jonathan Kozol

5

Moving On

The music throbbed through the wooden floor. The vibrations pulsed against Denzel's bare feet, moving, jumping, and beating in bursts of energy through his legs. With his eyes closed, he felt the music burning and bumping into his chest, over his muscles, and down through his arms, making his hands fly to the rhythms and jerk with the beats. With the music coursing through him, a flood of signs burst from his hands. The music was his heartbeat, the vibrations were his blood, and his hands ached with the beat of everything he'd ever wanted to say.

As the music pulsed away, Denzel stood still and quiet on the stage. He hesitantly opened his eyes. Without the pounding vibrations, the building suddenly seemed quiet, even to him. A second passed as he looked out over the audience. Then the students burst into applause. While some students clapped, others waved their hands in the air; still others beat their feet against the ground, making vibrations that Denzel could again feel. Even the students who didn't know American Sign Language (ASL) were clapping. A satisfied smile spread across Denzel's face as he took a bow and swaggered off stage. His friends had been skeptical when he told them he was going to rap in this year's talent show, but apparently they had liked it.

Denzel loved living in Rochester, New York. There were so many other deaf people here. He had plenty of friends in school, and there were lots of community programs for him to get involved in. Everything in his life seemed to have changed since his family moved to this new city. His parents were happier here, too. Since he was in high school now, his mom had gone back to work. In Rochester, she was able to work for a bigger newspaper than in the small town where they used to live. His dad also seemed happier. In the city, they had made friends with other parents of deaf children and weren't always fighting with the school to get fair treatment for Denzel.

Now that his mom had gone back to work, not only did she seem happier, but they had more money than they had before. Their first year in Rochester, Denzel got a personal computer for Christmas. Denzel hated using the telephone; it was so hard for him to hear the other person and very difficult for the other person to understand him. With his new computer, he could talk to his friends from his house. E-mail and instant messenger were like keys for unlocking a door to a whole new world of freedom.

When his mom went back to work, Denzel was also able to get a service dog. Groucho had to be the smartest, friendliest, and ugliest dog anyone ever met. He looked like a cross between a bulldog and a Chihuahua who had then been attacked by some crazed, chemical-wielding hairdresser. But Denzel felt that his ghastly looks and spiky, crimped hair were just part of Groucho's charm. Groucho wasn't pretty, but he sure was smart. He seemed to be able to do anything. If Denzel was alone in the house, Groucho listened for the telephone or doorbell to ring. If Denzel was out on the street, Groucho kept his ears open for cars or other dangers that Denzel might not hear. Groucho even understood sign language!

Sign language was another great thing about Rochester. When they moved to the city four years ago, Denzel was astonished to see so many people speaking in sign language. He immediately wanted to learn. He couldn't understand why his parents were so hesitant about letting him take classes. Taking matters into his own hands, Denzel started learning ASL from some friends at school. He was amazed by how easily his ASL-speaking friends spoke with each other. They never had to ask each other to speak more slowly or try to decipher each other's voices. They just said what they wanted to say with their hands. Suddenly Denzel felt like the odd one out—not because he couldn't hear but because he couldn't sign. Still, his parents resisted his pleas for classes, until they met Gerard.

Denzel met Gerard on a city bus. Groucho was sitting obediently at Denzel's feet, as he always did when they took the bus around the city. Gerard must have seen Denzel's hearing aid, because he touched Denzel's shoulder and signed, "I like your dog." Denzel had learned enough sign language to know what Gerard had said.

"Thank you," he signed back. Then added with a smile, "He's beautiful, don't you think?" Gerard laughed aloud. A few people on the bus turned to look at the sound of Gerard's laugh, but he didn't seem to care.

"What kind is he?" Gerard signed. Denzel didn't know if there was a sign for bulldog or Chihuahua so he fingerspelled the names. As Gerard continued to sign, Denzel got more and more lost. He told Gerard that he didn't know enough signs for their conversation and asked if Gerard spoke. Gerard smiled, shook his head, and took out a pad of paper. "Not well enough for you to lip-read." He smiled as he handed the notebook to Denzel, and Denzel smiled back as he read the sentence. For the rest of the bus ride, they continued to chat, now using the notebook to write things that Denzel couldn't understand or sign. As they talked, Denzel thought about how absurd it was that he and Gerard were both deaf and yet couldn't communicate with each other. Denzel told Gerard how much he wanted to learn ASL, but that his parents were skeptical. As it turned out, Gerard was a teacher of ASL, and by the time Denzel and Groucho reached their stop, Gerard had given Denzel his e-mail address and offered to give sign language lessons to Denzel *and* to his parents.

Once Denzel began learning sign language, he felt like a whole new world had opened up to him. He still spoke mostly aloud to his parents, but he felt a new sense of freedom with his closest friends. He didn't have to worry about them not understanding his words or, worse yet, laughing at the sound of his voice. At his school, he didn't have to worry about the teachers not accepting him, because there were other deaf students and most of the teachers had training in deaf education. There were even two teachers in his school who were deaf.

Being in Rochester was great because there were so many deaf people. Denzel felt like part of a real community. Studying with Gerard was wonderful because he helped both Denzel and his parents become part of the deaf community. And then there was something else great about living in Rochester and knowing Gerard. Gerard had a daughter named Gloria.

CLAPPING FOR DEAF PERFORMERS?

Just because Denzel is deaf doesn't mean he can't enjoy or participate in music. Denzel, like many deaf people, enjoys "listening" to music by turning it up loud and feeling the vibrations. But he doesn't just listen to music; he also raps using sign language. Many deaf people learn to play instruments and participate in music in various and creative ways. After Denzel's performance at his high school, many people clap, but other people wave their hands in the air. This is something that deaf people often do instead of clapping. A deaf person can't hear their audience clapping, but he can see the audience members waving their hands. Denzel can also feel the vibrations from the audience members stomping their feet. Their waving hands and stomping feet let him know that they enjoyed the show.

An audience made up of individuals who are deaf will find ways to express their appreciation.

A public telephone designed especially for people who are deaf.

THE DEAF COMMUNITY OF ROCHESTER, NEW YORK

Rochester, New York, has the largest *per capita* deaf population of any city in the United States. Because it has such a large deaf population, Rochester offers many programs and resources to deaf and hard-of-hearing people. It is one of the few cities in the country where one can see American Sign Language used widely outside of deaf classrooms. It offers many educational opportunities at schools like the Rochester School for the Deaf, the National Technical Institute for the Deaf at the Rochester Technical Institute, and the University of Rochester. Furthermore, there are many social and community organizations for deaf and hard-of-hearing people.

Any large city, however, will also have services for people who are deaf and hard of hearing. Washington, DC; Boston, Massachusetts; Austin, Texas; and Fremont, California also have sizeable populations of deaf and hard-of-hearing people. These cities offer many community and educational opportunities for this population that are similar to what Rochester has to offer.

HOW DO DEAF AND HARD-OF-HEARING PEOPLE USE THE TELEPHONE?

Did you know that Alexander Graham Bell, the inventor of the telephone, was a teacher of the deaf? In fact, he was working on inventing a hearing aid when he came up with the idea for the telephone. It is somewhat *ironic* then that his most famous invention was one that deaf people could not use. In the past, deaf and hard-of-hearing people often used teletypewriters (or TTYs) instead of telephones. A TTY works much like a fax machine. The person on one end types her message, and the person on the other end receives the message. Unfortunately, most deaf and hard-of-

Alexander Graham Bell, the inventor of the telephone, was also a teacher of the deaf.

hearing people could not afford TTYs, and both people had to have one in order to talk.

With improved hearing aids and cochlear implants, some deaf and hard-of-hearing people talk on regular telephones. Even more use e-mail and instant messaging to keep in touch. Cell phones with text messaging capabilities allow people to write to each other on the phone. Every day, advances in technology bring new worlds of communication options to deaf people.

HEARING-EAR DOGS?

Did you know that the average dog can hear two to three times better than the average human? Dogs can use their

Service dogs provide assistance to individuals with many forms of disability.

Guide dogs are usually German shepherds and retrievers, but hearing dogs can be any breed.

special hearing to help people in important ways. Just as many blind people have guide dogs, many deaf people have hearing dogs. Guide dogs are usually German shepherds and retrievers. They have to be big and strong to do their jobs. But hearing dogs, as long as they are friendly and highly intelligent, can be any kind of dog. Most hearing dogs are mixed-breed dogs who have been rescued from pounds and shelters. They go to hearing-dog school where they are trained to perform jobs and understand sign language. A hearing dog is trained to do things like wake his partner up when the alarm clock goes off, tell his partner when the phone or doorbell rings, and alert his partner to other noises like water boiling over on the stove or a baby crying.

FAMOUS FACES

Gideon E. (1842–1895) and
H. Humphrey (1844–1926) Moore

Brothers Gideon E. and H. Humphrey Moore were born in Philadelphia, Pennsylvania, and New York City respectively. After going deaf in his teenage years, Gideon went on to study at Yale College, was the first deaf American to earn his Ph.D., and became a famous chemist. His brother, H. Humphrey, became deaf at age three. While Gideon's passion was for the sciences, his brother's were for art. H. Humphrey Moore went on to be a famous painter in America and around the world.

Getting along with others isn't meant to be easy—it's hard work.
—Joan Meider

6

GLORIA

Denzel had never met anyone like Gloria before. Gloria was hearing, but her first language was ASL. Her parents, Gerard and Sylvia, were both deaf. However, both had become deaf from illnesses in childhood, so they fully expected to have a hearing child. Nevertheless, they had agreed long before Gloria was born that they would raise their child to speak their own language first and to speak English second.

Gloria amazed Denzel. He didn't know any other hearing person who spoke ASL so well. Gloria spoke it much better than he did, and often served as another teacher when Denzel said something wrong or didn't know a sign. Gloria spoke English with some of her other friends, but she signed so often that sometimes Denzel forgot that she could even hear. And sometimes this got him in trouble.

Even though Gloria had grown up in Deaf culture, she did not like to be stomped at or have the lights flashed to get her attention. Soon after she and Denzel started dating, Denzel made this mistake one too many times. They were sitting in his bedroom studying for a test. Gloria was sitting at the computer with her back to Denzel who was sitting on his bed. Groucho lay sleeping with his head on Denzel's knee. Not wanting to get up to get Gloria's attention, Denzel reached over and clicked his reading light on and off.

Gloria spun around in her chair. "Why did you do that?" she demanded, suddenly talking instead of signing. Groucho jolted awake and he looked up startled. Denzel didn't have his hearing aids in, but he could lip-read what she was saying. He was flabbergasted by her outburst.

"I wanted to get your attention," he said slowly and carefully, not knowing why she was so upset or why she wasn't signing.

"So why didn't you just say my name?" she demanded, then forcefully repeated herself in sign language.

"Hey," Denzel retorted, his voice very loud, "what's the big deal?" Now he was getting angry. Gloria's shoulders softened and she quickly stood up, walked to the bed, and sat down beside Denzel.

"Wait," she signed now, "I'm sorry. It's just that . . ." Gloria paused for a second to collect her thoughts. Then she returned to speaking aloud. "You know how we're always talking about how people have to respect Deaf culture?" Denzel watched her lips closely and nodded his head. Seeing how hard he had to concentrate, Gloria returned to signing. "I was raised in Deaf culture, but I can hear, so I'm part of hearing culture as well." She paused momentarily for emphasis. "I don't like it when people flash the lights or stomp at me. When my parents want my attention, they call my name. I can hear, and you can speak, so I wish you would just use my name if you want my attention." Gloria attempted to pick her words gently, but Denzel couldn't keep from getting angry.

"I don't know what your problem is, Gloria." Groucho lifted his ears, cocked his head to one side, and gave a confused whimper at the anger he heard in Denzel's voice. "I didn't do anything wrong!" Denzel thought he might be shouting, but he wasn't sure.

Gloria didn't wait around to find out if he intended for his tone to be so harsh. "Forget it," she said, as angry now as he was. "I'm going home." She grabbed her coat and walked out, Groucho following at her heels. The dog pulled his nose back just in time to avoid the slamming door.

Hours later, Denzel was still fuming over their conversation. *She knows I'm deaf, so why was she asking me to act like a hearing person?* he wondered to himself. At dinner that night, he related the event to his parents. "Can you believe that?" he asked after sharing the frustrating story. His parents looked at one another. They had been taking sign language classes with Denzel but weren't picking it up as quickly as he was. They still preferred their old communication method of speaking supplemented by cued speech. Denzel read their lips as they spoke.

"Well, you know, Denzel." His dad seemed to be picking his words carefully. "I think I understand where Gloria is coming from." Denzel's eyebrows went up. This was not quite the reaction he had expected. He had expected them to be on his side. He looked toward his mom, but she was inspecting the food on her plate, avoiding looking up. "To be perfectly honest, Denzel," his father continued, "your mom and I haven't liked your foot stomping or light flashing much either." Denzel opened his mouth to protest, but Roger lifted a hand. "It's not that we don't understand—we do. We know it's the way that you and your friends, Gerard, and your teachers do things, and that's fine. But it's not the way we raised you to do things here."

"Denzel, honey—" Denzel's mom placed her hand over Roger's and broke into the conversation. "We're not saying that it upsets us."

Denzel hated it when she called him "honey." He was sixteen years old, for crying out loud. How long was she going to keep doing that? And why was everyone turning on him? Dana paid no heed to the look on Denzel's face and continued.

"We're just saying that it's something that we've noticed. You used to call to us aloud and talk to us more. Since you got your computer and have been learning sign language, well, it's just been a lot quieter around here." Denzel looked from his mother's face to his father's face and back again. What was everyone's problem today? Had everyone forgotten that he was deaf? When did everyone get the nerve to tell him how he should act? His mom looked at him, and it was like she could read his mind "It's not that we're telling you how you should act," she continued. "All we're saying is that it's nice to be called 'Mom' and 'Dad' once in a while."

For the rest of dinner, glasses and silverware clinked, but everything else was silent. As soon as dinner was over, Denzel went to his room to think. He wanted to stay angry, but the more he thought about it, the more he understood what his mom, dad, and Gloria were saying. Of all the hearing people he'd known, they were the only three who always made the effort to talk to him in the way he preferred and could most easily understand. They were always concerned about his feelings and his needs. If all they wanted from him was for him to use his voice once in a while to call them by their names, was that really so hard?

The next morning, Denzel saw Gloria at the far end of the crowded school hallway. She hadn't been on instant messenger the night before, and he was pretty sure she was still mad. Students pushed against him as he stood waving his hand, trying to catch Gloria's eye. She didn't see him, turned her back, and began walking in the opposite direction through the sea of people. Yesterday, Denzel would have let her walk away and just talked to her when he saw her in school later, but he knew she didn't want him to do that. He gathered his courage and opened his mouth,

"Gloria!" he shouted over the heads of the other students. She didn't turn around. Feeling suddenly self-conscious, he wondered if he was loud enough. "Gloria!" he called again, this time forcing more air through his throat, but she still didn't turn around. Was she ignoring him, or could she not recognize her name coming from his unusual voice? She was nearly to the end of the hall, so he concentrated on using as much air as he could and called out a third time, "Gloria!" This time many people turned to give Denzel a look, but he didn't notice. His eyes were locked with Gloria's as she came striding toward him with a big smile on her face.

TYPES OF HEARING LOSS

Both of Gloria's parents are deaf, yet she is hearing. Both of Denzel's parents are hearing, but he is deaf. How can this be?

Hearing loss can be caused by many different things and can occur at any time in life. Although there are many different types of hearing loss, they can be grouped into two main categories. They are *genetic* and *nongenetic* hearing loss.

Genetic Hearing Loss

Genetic hearing loss runs in a family. Thirty percent of children with hearing loss have a genetic hearing loss. This

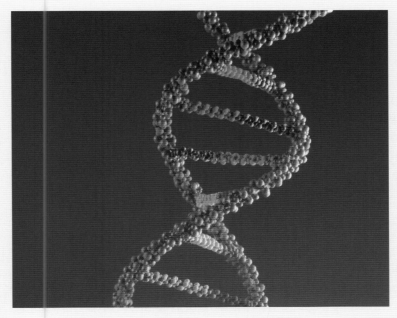

A strand of DNA may hold the answers to genetic forms of hearing loss.

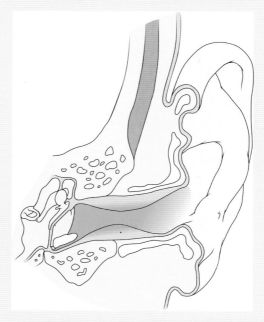

Some hearing loss is caused by middle ear defects.

means that one or both of the parents had a ***gene***, or ***hereditary*** characteristic, for hearing loss that they passed down to the child. When the child was first formed, either the egg from the mother or the sperm from the father carried information that would cause the new child to form without normal hearing.

Even if no one in a family had hearing loss in the past, a child can still be born with a genetic hearing loss. This can happen because of a gene ***mutation***. This would mean that the genetic information in the parents did not originally contain any information that would cause hearing loss in their children. However, the information that is passed in the egg or sperm mutates or changes from its original form. This can happen for different reasons. Perhaps the parents were exposed to a chemical, illness, or something dangerous in the environment. Perhaps when the information in the egg and sperm joined, the information changed for an unknown reason. Whatever the cause for the mutation, the genes changed, causing the child to develop with altered hearing. This newly formed genetic trait is now a part of his genes, and he can pass these genes on to his own children.

Nongenetic Hearing Loss

Seventy percent of children with hearing loss have a non-genetic hearing loss. This means that the information contained in the child's genes is normal but that some outside

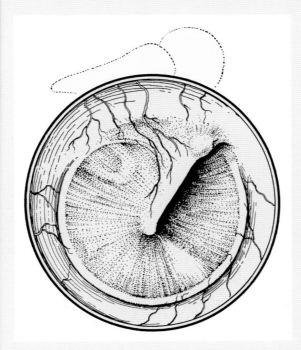

The eardrum is just one of the parts necessary for hearing.

A child's hearing loss may be caused by many things.

factor affected her body or her mother's body resulting in a hearing loss. Many different things can cause a nongenetic hearing loss. For example, perhaps the pregnant mother took medication or other types of drugs that affected the body of the developing baby. If a pregnant mother gets a certain type of illness, like **cytomegalovirus** or **toxoplasmosis**, it can sometimes cause hearing loss in the baby. Children born with normal hearing can also contract illnesses that cause hearing loss. Illnesses like **meningitis**, certain medications, and premature birth or other difficulties in the birth process can all affect the delicate ear structure and nerves of a newborn baby, causing permanent hearing loss.

Illnesses can cause children born with normal hearing to become deaf.

Deaf OR deaf?

Sometimes you will see the word "Deaf" capitalized while other times it is spelled "deaf." Deaf is capitalized when it refers to people who see themselves as part of "Deaf culture." It is not capitalized when it refers to deafness as a medical condition.

RELATIONSHIPS

Clear communication is one of the most important elements of any successful relationship. Romantic and other **_interpersonal_** relationships can pose unique challenges to people who are deaf and hard of hearing—especially if their relationship is with a hearing person who does not under-

A Halloween party at the Rochester School for the Deaf helps young students build strong interpersonal skills.

stand deaf issues or Deaf culture. Gloria was raised in Deaf culture and understands the things Denzel goes through. Nevertheless, because they have different backgrounds and different ways of doing things (as would any two individuals, deaf or non-deaf), they still have to negotiate and compromise to make their relationship work (as is the case with all relationships).

All successful relationships involve **negotiation** and compromise, but these things can be difficult if the two people have different communication methods. Imagine trying to have the conversation that Gloria and Denzel had with a person who doesn't speak your language. How would you make yourself understood? How would you understand the other person? How could you tell the other person what you were feeling without offending him? Would you expect that person to learn to understand your language without trying to understand his? This is a problem that deaf and hard-of-hearing people face with hearing people every day. Most hearing people expect deaf people to learn their language but don't make any attempt to learn the deaf person's language in return.

Do hearing people have the "right" to expect deaf people to use their voices and follow the social customs of hearing people? Apparently, this is what Gloria believes. Do you think she is right?

Communicating with Hearing Parents

Some hearing parents of a deaf child resist teaching their child sign language because they don't want her growing up speaking a different language from them. However, no matter what method of education they choose, hearing parents often face difficulties communicating with their deaf child. They may feel sorrowful that their relationship with their child is not as close as they would like it to be, or they

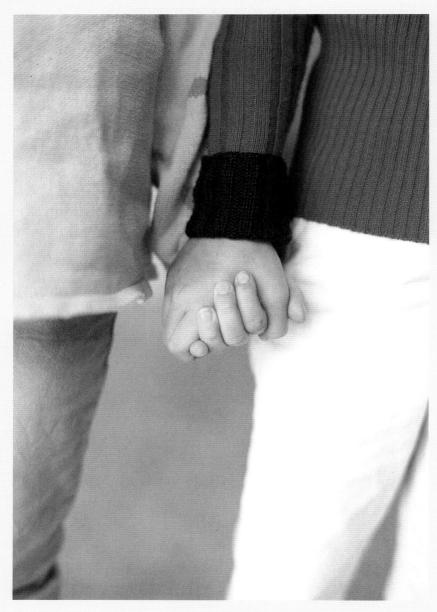

Some forms of communication require no ears.

may feel that other people (like sign language teachers or their child's deaf friends) know their child better than they do. Many deaf education programs focus not only on teaching deaf children to communicate but also on teaching parents how to understand and interact with their children.

FAMOUS FACES

Granville Seymour Redmond (1871–1935)

You may be surprised to know that deaf people have performed in American film from its very beginnings. Born in Philadelphia, Pennsylvania, Granville Seymour Redmond became deaf after suffering from scarlet fever when he was a toddler. Seymour received his education in California and in Paris, France. He became a visual artist and a silent film actor. He worked closely with Charlie Chaplin and encouraged other deaf people to pursue a life in the arts.

There is a time for departure, even when there's no certain place to go.
—Tennessee Williams

7

Some Things Can't Last

Driving through the tall, wrought iron gates was like entering another world. The car followed the winding path past towering stone buildings and under a canopy of green branches. Activity hummed all around. Movement coursed through the grounds. Students sat in colorful bunches and balls flew in friendly games. The very buildings seemed animated with breath, and everything felt completely, wonderfully alive. But what made all the activity, all the movement even more wonderful was the striking contrast—for all around people were talking, laughing, playing, and studying, yet everything was peacefully but strangely quiet.

This was Gallaudet University in Washington, D.C. Roger and Dana sat in the front of the van, and Denzel, Gloria, Gerard, and Sylvia sat crammed among boxes, bags, and computer cords in the back. Gerard and Sylvia had met on this very campus, and Gloria had always planned on studying here to become a teacher for the deaf. Rochester had many great schools where Denzel could have attended college, but once Gloria told him about Gallaudet, Denzel didn't want to go anywhere else.

The first weeks at Gallaudet were the best of Denzel's life. Even in Rochester, he had never been in such a concentration of deaf people before. There were also hearing students on the campus, but all of them were there because they cared about deafness. Best of all, everyone spoke sign language! No matter how much Gloria had talked about Gallaudet and described what it would be like, Denzel hadn't been able to really imagine it. Now, he couldn't believe they were finally here.

Denzel still suffered at times from not being a ***native speaker*** of ASL, but every day at college, his ASL improved. He had also never been quite as good in school as Gloria was. In college there was a lot more work, the work was harder, and there were more opportunities to get distracted and go have fun. This wasn't always the best combination for Denzel, and he often relied on Gloria to give him extra help when he didn't understand something or when he fell behind.

By the end of their first year at Gallaudet, Denzel began noticing that something was different about Gloria. He never asked her about it and tried to pretend it wasn't there, but as the summer approached, an unknown fear began to whisper in the back of his mind. She rarely stopped by his dorm to meet him anymore. She was hardly ever on instant messenger when he signed on. She came late to their dates, and even sometimes forgot. When they had first arrived at Gallaudet, they had loved going into the city and walking around the monuments together. Now the cherry trees were blossoming and springtime filled the air, but Gloria hardly ever wanted to go with Denzel to the city at all. He tried to tell himself that finals were approaching and Gloria was really busy, but he feared it was something more.

One evening, Gloria told Denzel she couldn't meet him for coffee because she had to study late at the library. He thought he'd surprise her by smuggling some coffee into the library and studying with her there. On his way to the coffee shop, he passed the bus stop. He glanced over as the bus pulled up. Gloria was getting off the bus. Denzel smiled and lifted his arm to wave. Then he stopped. Someone else was getting off with her. Without knowing why, Denzel took two steps back, stepped gingerly behind a lamppost, and hoped that Gloria wouldn't see him. The stranger, whoever he was, took Gloria's hand and led her across campus. After a few feet, she dropped her hand, but he gently picked it up again. Denzel let them get a little distance away, and then with his heart in his throat, he followed.

The young man leaned against a red brick building, and Gloria stepped toward him. Her back was to Denzel, and her hands rested behind her. Denzel could see the young man's lips moving, but he was too far away to see what he was saying. Gloria leaned her shoulder against the wall and swept her hair from her face. Denzel watched tensely, trying to catch something from their flying lips. Since coming to Gallaudet, he hardly ever saw Gloria talking to people without using sign language. Watching her talk like this, leaning against the wall, hands clasped behind her back, was almost like watching a stranger.

Denzel couldn't read their lips, but he could certainly read their body language. Gloria gave the young man lingering glances as she spoke, glances that Denzel hadn't seen in a long time. She gravitated toward him as he talked, and he nudged her playfully with his elbow. The young man **gesticulated** meaninglessly with his hands as he spoke. Denzel looked at him with contempt. Watching his motions, Denzel was sure that this man did not know sign language. Gloria touched the man's arm and laughed. Bile rose in Denzel's throat.

Then the man touched his fingers to Gloria's chin and leaned in to kiss her. Looking at the ground, Gloria stepped back and shook her head. The young man didn't look discouraged and reached toward her face again. This time, Gloria slapped his hand away and started signing fast. "Why do you do this?" she said. "You know I can't." Denzel understood what she was saying, but the young man didn't. He reached out to quiet Gloria's hands. For a painful moment, Gloria looked into the young man's eyes. As they stood unmoving, Denzel realized he was holding his breath. Then Gloria pulled her hands from the young man's, signed, "I'm sorry," and began walking away.

Looking like he'd been punched, the man closed his eyes and slumped against the wall. He seemed to be moving in slow motion as he sank to a sitting position and put his head between his knees. Denzel finally released his breath in one long, relieved sigh. As he looked at the young man cradling his head in his hands, Denzel felt a sense of triumph. He looked in the direction Gloria had gone and thought about following her.

Gloria had not gone far. She too was watching the young man sitting against the wall. Denzel's sense of triumph quickly dissipated as Gloria walked back toward the red brick building. Looking sorrowful and broken, she sank down beside the man and whispered into his ear. The young man lifted his head slowly, and when he did, Gloria cupped his face in her hands and kissed him. Then she laid her forehead upon his shoulder. Her own shoulders shook as she began to cry. Denzel could not watch anymore. He turned his back and walked away.

That night, Denzel waited outside of Gloria's dorm. It was eleven o'clock when he saw her finally walking up the path. He did not stand to greet her, and she did not rush to embrace him. Instead she sat down beside him and began to sign.

"We need to talk."

"So who is he?" Denzel broke in.

Gloria's eyes widened at his question, then her shoulders slumped. "You know?"

Denzel wanted to say more, but he simply nodded. They sat still for a moment. Then Gloria began to sign again.

"I wish you didn't know," she continued, "but you need to understand that it's not about him."

Quick anger jumped in Denzel's throat. "What do you mean it's not about him?" Denzel signed furiously. "I saw you today. I know what it's about."

"Denzel," Gloria broke in, "I'm not coming back to Gallaudet next year." Denzel sat back, stunned. All through the evening as he waited for Gloria, he had been preparing for something terrible, but he had not prepared for this.

"All my life I wanted to come to Gallaudet and become a sign language teacher like my dad," Gloria went on, trying desperately to make Denzel understand. "But it's not what I expected. I don't fit in here. And as much as we tried, I don't think I fit with you. I don't know who I am, but when we're together now, I feel like I'm always trying to be someone I'm not."

Denzel could not believe what Gloria was saying. They had been inseparable for years. His world was crumbling all around him, and he was totally unprepared for the collapse. Suddenly, all his fears and misgivings made sense. But despite those fears, he hadn't seen this coming. He wondered with bewilderment how he could not have seen the signs before.

Tears streamed down Gloria's face. "Loving someone shouldn't be so difficult."

Denzel read her lips and spoke back in a strangled, frantic voice, "But it's not difficult." His words slurred together with emotion. Then, in a desperate effort to reach Gloria and change her mind, Denzel said in clear, careful words, "I didn't have to try to love you. It just happened. Every morning I wake up loving you without even thinking!"

Gloria was silent as she wiped the tears from her face. When she spoke again, it was again in sign. "You're right, Denzel. It's not difficult to love you. It's easy to love you."

For a brief moment, Denzel felt relieved by her words, but then Gloria touched his arm and continued. "It's not difficult to love you, but it is difficult to date you . . . too difficult." Gloria held her hands up in sad frustration, and then simply signed, "I hope we can still be friends."

But as he watched her slip away into the dorm, Denzel knew they would not be friends, and a weight settled like a stone in his heart.

THE BILINGUAL-BICULTURAL APPROACH

Even though Gloria was born hearing, her Deaf parents raised her using the bilingual-bicultural approach (or Bi-Bi) to education. In Bi-Bi, deaf and hard-of-hearing children grow up learning a visual sign language as their primary language. Bi-Bi's goal is to provide full language development that leads to mastery of English as a second language, so that students can function in both the Deaf and hearing worlds. In the United States and English-speaking Canada, this language is American Sign Language (ASL). In Québec (the French-speaking province of Canada), this language is La Langue des Signes Québecoise (LSQ). Denmark and Sweden have Danish Sign Language, and China has Chinese Sign Language. In fact, most countries have a sign language that is native to that land and is a separate language from what hearing people speak.

Many people think ASL is just English made into signs. However, it is actually a different language from English. There is a type of sign language called Manually Coded English (MCE), in which a person signs the exact English words she is speaking, but ASL is different. A child who is raised "speaking" ASL does not automatically know English. ASL-speaking children learn English as a second language in the same way that English-speaking children learn French, Spanish, Japanese, or any other second language.

Deaf and hard-of-hearing people who use the Bi-Bi approach refer to themselves as being part of Deaf culture. They believe that when you are deaf and speak ASL, you are actually part of a different culture from hearing people. For example, in Deaf culture certain behaviors like stomping your foot, hitting your hand on a table, or flashing the lights to get a person's attention are considered not only acceptable but also helpful and appropriate. In hearing society, people consider these actions rude. Since hearing people

People who are part of the Deaf culture may have their own sports teams.

Students who are deaf and hard of hearing enjoy using computers.

generally know very little about deaf people or Deaf culture, they often misunderstand deaf people's actions. Advocates of the Bi-Bi approach think it is very important that deaf children learn sign language and become part of the Deaf community where they will be fully accepted and won't always struggle to be understood and to fit in. Children raised in the Bi-Bi approach usually attend schools for the deaf where ASL is used as the method of communication. The Learning Center for Deaf Children in Framingham, Massachusetts, is one of the only non-college schools that practices this

Children who have grown up using Bi-Bi will often attend special schools like the Rochester School for the Deaf. There they can participate in many activities.

Thomas Gallaudet was a groundbreaking teacher of students with hearing loss.

method. The Bi-Bi approach is also the educational method used by Gallaudet University.

GALLAUDET UNIVERSITY

Located in Washington, D.C., Gallaudet University is one of the only universities in the world where deaf, hard-of-hearing, and hearing students can attend all their classes, receive their education, and earn their degree in sign language. Unlike many other schools for the deaf, not only are the majority of the students deaf or hard of hearing at Gallaudet but many of the professors and administrators are deaf or hard of hearing as well. Gallaudet is now known around the world for its unique community, education, and work to improve the lives of deaf people everywhere.

FAMOUS FACES

Gertrude Scott Galloway (born in 1930)

Born in Washington, D.C., Gertrude Scott Galloway has dedicated her life to teaching and activism. Her parents, grandparents, brothers, and sisters were all born deaf, so Galloway was immersed in Deaf culture from the moment she was born. She studied at Gallaudet University and later became a teacher for the deaf. She also became a history maker when in 1982 she was elected as the first deaf woman president of the National Association for the Deaf.

Hope is not a dream, but a way of
making dreams become reality.
—L. J. Cardina Suenens

8

THE OCEAN INSIDE

The wave tumbled and broke over Denzel's skin in a rush of foam and spray. Eyes closed, he felt the water splashing against his face and churning in his ears. He held his breath as the receding water trickled down his neck and the sand and pebbles shifted beneath his skin. Then he took another deep breath and waited for the next wave to flow over him. Immersed in the rhythmic feeling of the water, Denzel thought about how far he'd come in the last three years.

That first summer back in Rochester was torture for Denzel. Every day he woke up thinking about Gloria. He moped around the house and snapped at his parents. He had done terribly on his finals and had been placed on academic probation. Even Groucho could tell something was wrong and followed at Denzel's heels like a miniature version of Denzel's ugly mood.

Dana and Roger didn't know what to do for their son. In years past, they would have called Gerard and Sylvia to ask for advice, but since Denzel and Gloria broke up, they couldn't even do that. Worst of all, Denzel didn't want to go back to Gallaudet. He kept saying all it would do was remind him of Gloria.

When Denzel hadn't snapped out of his stormy mood by the

end of the summer, Dana and Roger decided it was time for some "tough love." They tried to assure Denzel that they understood what he was going through, that they were always going to be there for him. But they also told him that there was no way he was going to quit Gallaudet without giving it another shot.

"Honey," Dana began as Denzel groaned, "you've never been out on your own before. You've always had your father and me to support you, and you always had Gerard, Sylvia, and Gloria to help you. Your father and I just think it's time you got out on your own without us or Gloria." She cued the words as she spoke them.

Roger said simply, "Denzel, it's time to sink or swim."

That first semester back at Gallaudet, Denzel was sure he was sinking. He couldn't concentrate on classes, and without Gloria to help him study, his grades slipped even further behind. When he came home for Christmas break, he figured his next semester would be his last at Gallaudet.

Denzel couldn't say exactly when things changed, but sometime in the spring, as the flowers were just starting to break through the soil and as the cherry trees were beginning to bud, Denzel felt the cloud in his life parting as well. Finally, a little bit of sunshine was poking through. He worked harder at school, his grades improved, and he started looking into clubs to join. That summer, instead of going home to think about Gloria, Denzel worked at an internship in a Washington, D.C., children's center. While working there, he came up with an idea for a student club of his own.

He called his club "Building Bridges." In Building Bridges, pairs of deaf or hard-of-hearing college students acted as **mentors** for deaf, hard-of-hearing, and hearing children. Denzel loved how Gallaudet brought deaf, hard-of-hearing, and hearing people together, and he wanted his club to do the same thing for kids. Each pair of students mentored a pair of kids. The pairs were made up of one deaf or hard-or-hearing child and one hearing child. Twice a month, the mentors met their kids to work on homework, do a community service project, or just plain have fun. Over the next year, the group became more successful than

Denzel could have imagined, and Denzel felt a new enthusiasm for everything he did.

Now Denzel was in his senior year at Gallaudet and looking forward to graduation. He still wasn't sure what he was going to do after college, but he knew that he wanted to stay in Washington, D.C., and continue Building Bridges.

This year his mentoring partner was a woman named Caroline. At the beginning of the year, Denzel had been very suspicious of Caroline. She didn't go to Gallaudet; she was a senior at George Washington University. She had been raised with the auditory-verbal approach to education that Denzel's parents had first tried on him. She had a cochlear implant and had received her early education at a school in Massachusetts called the Clarke School for the Deaf. She didn't even know sign language! But when he saw how well she worked with Julian and Becky, the children they were assigned to mentor, Denzel's fears subsided. In fact, he soon found that he and Caroline actually made the perfect pair when it came to communicating with Julian (who was hard of hearing) and Becky (who was hearing). After spending so much time sad and alone, Denzel finally felt like he belonged and that there were good things ahead.

Denzel's thoughts returned to the feeling of the cold water mixing with the warm sun on his skin. As the water rushed over him, Caroline grabbed his arm. Denzel sat up, and the wave tumbled around his waist. Caroline flew up with a gasp and spit a mouthful of salty water back into the ocean. Denzel pointed at her and laughed. She retaliated with a shove that sent Denzel sprawling face first into the water and sand. This time Caroline laughed as Denzel came up gasping. She yelped as he pulled her back into the sand and desperately mouthed the word "truce" as another wave rushed into their faces. They both sat up laughing and turned to check on the kids. Julian and Becky were engrossed in building a sand castle.

Caroline and Denzel looked out across the water, and Caroline lifted her hands. "I think it sounds like that," she signed. "I think the ocean sounds like the feeling of the water as it rushes over your skin." Her hands spoke in fluid movements. "I think it's like if you could make that feeling of the water, stones, and sand rolling against each other . . . I think it would be like feeling that inside your ears."

Denzel stared at her. "You signed all that!" he spoke aloud. "When did you learn that?"

"Oh, I've been taking lessons," Caroline replied with a grin. "What do you think?"

Denzel hardly knew what to say. "I think it's great!"

"No," Caroline laughed. "I mean what do you think about the ocean? How do you think it sounds?"

Denzel paused and looked out over the water. He thought about how, as a child, he used to hold his hand to his father's throat to feel him singing. He turned so Caroline could see his lips. "I think you're right. I bet it sounds just like that." Then he added, "But I still don't see how all that sound can be trapped in a little seashell."

He was talking about something Becky had told them earlier. She had bought a shell at a store on the beach and kept holding it up to her ear. When Julian asked her what she was doing, she replied simply, "I can hear the ocean inside." This made Julian upset. He thought Becky was picking on him, because he couldn't hear like she could. But Becky was insistent that she really could hear the ocean inside of the shell. Even though Caroline had a cochlear implant and had more hearing than either Denzel or Julian, she couldn't hear anything in the shell. Finally, feeling exasperated, Becky had stormed over to a stranger on the beach and asked him to say what he heard in the shell.

"The ocean." The stranger shrugged and walked away.

Becky and Julian soon forgot their squabble. As they worked on building a sandcastle, Caroline and Denzel pondered this mystery of the ocean within a shell.

"I wonder what it sounds like," Denzel had mused aloud. Since Caroline had gone to an auditory-verbal school and grew up using her residual hearing, she hadn't known sign language, so Denzel almost always spoke to her aloud.

"You can hear it with your hearing aids, can't you?" Caroline had asked. She cued as she spoke. Since meeting Denzel a year ago, she had been learning and perfecting cuing because she knew he couldn't hear much of her voice and relied on lip-reading a lot.

"Well, yeah, I guess so," Denzel replied. "But I know it's not the way it really sounds. I mean, I wish I knew what it sounds like to other people who don't have to hear it through hearing aids or cochlear implants, you know?"

As they sat thinking about the ocean's noise inside the shell, Caroline reached up, removed the external part of her cochlear implant from the back of her head, and placed it on the beach towel. Denzel held his breath as she gently took the hearing aids from his ears. Without the hearing aids, everything went quiet. Then Caroline took Denzel's hand and led him out into the water. They lay side-by-side in the sand and allowed the water to rush over their bodies. They couldn't hear the ocean with their ears, but they could feel its vibration inside their bodies.

Denzel and Caroline emerged from the water and walked toward Julian and Becky. Becky nudged Julian in the ribs and pointed at Caroline and Denzel. They were holding hands. Becky and Julian giggled to one another; this had never happened before, and they were curious to see what would happen next. But Denzel and Caroline just came over and said it was time to pack up for the long drive back to Washington. Becky and Julian groaned.

Driving back to Washington, Denzel couldn't stop thinking about the conversation he and Caroline had in the sand. They had known each other for almost a year now, but they'd never talked like that before. Denzel wondered at the unfamiliar nervousness in his stomach and thought about how beautifully Caroline had signed earlier in the day. Normally, after a day with the kids, Caroline and Denzel said goodbye to each other and returned to their apartments near their separate schools. But tonight, after dropping the kids off at their parents' houses, Denzel lingered in Caroline's car, trying to think of things to talk about. Finally, feeling pathetic, he gulped down his fear and blurted out, "Caroline, would you like to go to a movie or something?"

Caroline smiled as she signed her reply. "I thought you were never going to ask."

COCHLEAR IMPLANTS: WHAT THEY ARE AND HOW THEY WORK

In 1990, the United States Food and Drug Administration approved cochlear implants for use in children. Since then, thousands of children worldwide have received the implant in the hope of gaining better hearing and speech abilities. A cochlear implant is an electronic device that is meant to do the job of a damaged or malfunctioning cochlea. Cochlear implants are not appropriate for everyone. Only people with certain types of hearing loss will benefit from cochlear implants.

The cochlear implant has both internal and external parts. A person with a cochlear implant has an attachment

A student at the Clarke School for the Deaf uses a cochlear implant. The external part of the implant is visible where it is attached above his ear.

Whether a child with hearing loss uses a cochlear implant, wears a hearing aid, or participates fully in the Deaf community, she will be capable of reaching out to the world around her.

on the outside of her head (this external part of the cochlear implant is often covered up by a person's hair). This is the microphone that amplifies sound. Surgically implanted beneath the person's scalp is an instrument that receives the sounds from the microphone and turns them into electrical signals. This instrument is about three inches long and is hidden beneath the skin. The microphone and receiver are attached together either by a powerful magnet or by a "button" or "snap" that comes out through the person's scalp. The receiver sends the electrical signals along a wire-like structure that goes into the cochlea. The wire-like structure sends the electrical impulses to the auditory nerve. The auditory nerve relays these impulses to the brain, which registers them as sound.

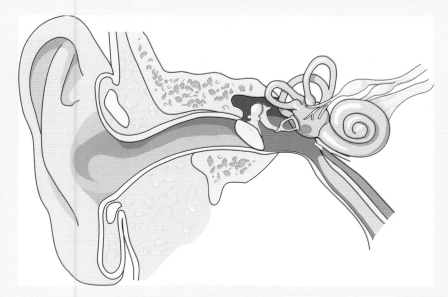

Normally, the outer ear "collects" sounds, but a cochlear implant receives the sound and turns it into an electrical signal that is transmitted to the auditory nerve, deep within the ear.

Hearing aids amplify sound. This is helpful for some types of hearing loss, but for a person with a malfunctioning cochlea, it won't matter how loud you make the sound because the cochlea still won't be able to transmit that sound to the auditory nerve. In cases like these, cochlear implants are a vast improvement on hearing aids and have changed many people's lives. However, it is still important to realize that cochlear implants are not cures for deafness. They cannot give a person "normal" hearing, and they cannot transmit all sounds. Although hearing aids and cochlear implants are amazing devices, modern technology still can't come close to replicating the incredible human ear.

Within the Deaf community there is controversy about the use of cochlear implants. Many feel that cochlear implants imply that Deaf individuals were "less than perfect" before they improved their hearing—as if hearing people are better than deaf people.

CLARKE SCHOOL FOR THE DEAF

Located in Northampton, Massachusetts, The Clarke School for the Deaf/Center for Oral Education began in 1867. It was the first oral institute (meaning that it taught children to communicate through verbal speech rather than through sign language) in the United States and remains one of the leading oral institutions in the world. The Clarke School uses the auditory-verbal method to teach children between the ages of birth and fifteen years old. Children attending the school learn to listen and speak. The children are then mainstreamed into schools with their hearing peers. The Clarke School now has **satellite** campuses in Philadelphia, Pennsylvania; Boston, Massachusetts; Jacksonville, Florida; and New York City.

President John F. Kennedy spends time with children at the Clarke School for the Deaf in Massachusetts.

FORMING RELATIONSHIPS

It would be easy to say that Denzel and Gloria's relationship did not work out because she is hearing and he is deaf—and that Denzel and Caroline's relationship did work because they were both deaf. However, people from very separate backgrounds can have successful relationships despite their differences—and people who come from the same backgrounds may fail to form long-term relationships.

Successful relationships involve both emotional and practical give-and-take. Denzel's relationship with Gloria may have been built too much on his dependency on her. Gloria was not only his girlfriend; she was also in many ways his teacher. As a result, Gloria may not have felt that she was free to grow and explore aspects of herself. In his relationship with Caroline, Denzel is more of an equal; they both have things to give to each other and they both have things to learn from each other.

When two people are very different, those differences can form the basis for mutual growth. But that only happens when we're willing to listen to each other—whether we use our ears or our eyes to do that. Good communication is the cornerstone of respect and understanding.

Bringing Deaf and Hearing People Together

More and more people are realizing that it should not just be up to deaf people to learn to function in hearing society; hearing people should learn about Deaf culture and what they can do to bridge the language and cultural gap that often exists between hearing and deaf/hard-of-hearing people. Denzel wants to help bridge that gap by developing a mentoring program that brings deaf and hearing children together with deaf role models. Many deaf schools now have preschool programs in which deaf and hearing

A hearing child listens for the ocean inside a seashell—but those who are deaf or hard of hearing feel the rhythm of the waves with their entire bodies.

children learn and play together. As time goes by, more and more hearing people are realizing that they and their children can learn and benefit from the experiences and communication methods of deaf people.

TOTAL COMMUNICATION

In the total communication method of deaf education, children are taught to use all their senses and all methods available to them to gain the best understanding of what is being said around them. A person using total communication may have hearing aids to help her hear better, use signs, speak with her voice, and lip-read. In total communication, you may see a person using MCE as he speaks aloud or even mixing ASL with speech. A person raised in the total communication method might sometimes rely only on sign language and might in other situations only use her listening and lip-reading skills. A child using total communication might attend a school for the deaf where total communication is used or might be mainstreamed into a school with hearing children. By the end of Denzel's story, we see that he has adopted a method of total communication in order to communicate with deaf, hard-of-hearing, and hearing people alike.

FAMOUS FACES

Marlee Matlin (born in 1965)

Marlee Matlin was born in Illinois and became deaf after an illness she suffered when she was eighteen months old. This has not stopped her from becoming a famous actress. You may have seen her in many television and film roles. During her career she has played characters ranging from a deaf lawyer in the television series *Reasonable Doubts*, to a deaf rabbit in *Disney's Adventures in Wonderland*. In 1986, Marlee Matlin received the Academy Award for Best Actress for her performance in the film *Children of a Lesser God*. She was both the first deaf actress and the youngest actress ever to receive this honor.

FURTHER READING

Biderman, Beverly. *Wired for Sound: A Journey into Hearing*. Markham, Ont.: Trifolium Books Inc., 1998.

Christensen, Kathee M., and Gilbert L. Delgado. *Multicultural Issues in Deafness*. White Plains, N.Y.: Longman Publishing Group, 1993.

Cohen, Leah Hager. *Train Go Sorry: Inside a Deaf World*. New York: Vintage Books, 1995.

Davis, Lennard J. *My Sense of Silence: Memoirs of a Childhood with Deafness*. Champaign: University of Illinois Press, 2000.

Farley, Cynthia. *Bridge to Sound with a 'Bionic' Ear*: Wayzata, Minn.: Periscope Press, 2002.

Lane, Harlan. *When the Mind Hears: A History of the Deaf*. New York: Random House, 1989.

————. *The Mask of Benevolence: Disabling the Deaf Community*. New York: Random House, 1992.

————, Robert Hoffmeister, and Ben Bahan. *A Journey into the Deaf-World*. San Diego, Calif.: Dawn Sign Press, 1996.

Lang, Harry G., and Bonnie Meath-Lang. *Deaf Persons in the Arts and Sciences: A Biographical Dictionary*. Westport, Conn.: Greenwood Press, 1995.

Marschark, Marc. *Raising and Educating a Deaf Child: A Comprehensive Guide to the Choices, Controversies, and Decisions Faced by Parents and Educators*. New York: Oxford University Press, 1997.

Schwartz, Sue. *Choices in Deafness: A Parents' Guide to Communication Options,* Second Edition. Bethesda, Md.: Woodbine House, 1996.

Spradley, Thomas S., and James P. Spradley. *Deaf Like Me*. Washington, D.C.: Gallaudet University Press, 1985.

Walker, Lou Ann. *A Loss for Words: The Story of Deafness in a Family*. New York: HarperCollins, 1987.

FOR MORE INFORMATION

Alexander Graham Bell Association for the Deaf and Hard of Hearing
www.agbell.org

Clarke School for the Deaf/Center for Oral Education
www.clarkeschool.org

The Deaf Community of Rochester, NY
www.deafrochester.com

Gallaudet University
www.gallaudet.edu

Hearing Dogs for Deaf People—Links
hearingdogs.orcon.net.nz/links

National Association of the Deaf
www.nad.org

National Technical Institute for the Deaf
ntidweb.rit.edu

Publisher's Note:

The Web sites listed on these pages were active at the time of publication. The publisher is not responsible for Web sites that have changed their address or discontinued operation since the date of publication. The publisher will review and update the Web sites upon each reprint.

GLOSSARY

amplifies: Makes greater or increases.

audiological: Having to do with one's sense of hearing.

audiologist: A doctor or technician who studies hearing and/or treats hearing loss.

bicultural: Being a member of two different cultures.

bilingual: Able to speak two languages.

cultural: Representative of or coming from the behaviors, beliefs, customs, arts, and institutions of a particular group or society.

cytomegalovirus: Any one of a certain group of herpes viruses that attack the tissue cells that cover internal and external organs.

expulsion: Forced out.

gene: Information passed from parent to child that will determine what characteristics the child will have.

gesticulated: Motioned or gestured to emphasize a point.

hereditary: Passed on from parent to offspring.

integrates: Brings together different things into one unit or whole.

interpersonal: Involving other people.

interpreters: People who can translate one language into another language or can clearly explain things that have been said so that others can understand it.

ironic: Contrary or opposite of what would be expected.

malformation: Something that is not formed in the correct way.

meningitis: A very serious bacterial or viral infection that causes fever, vomiting, intense headache, stiff neck, and can result in death.

mentors: People who teach other people, especially by leading through example.

molecules: The smallest particles that elements and compounds can be divided into before their chemical or physical properties change.

mutation: An alteration or change from something's original form.

native speaker: Speaking a language from birth.

negotiation: Working with others to come to an agreement.

per capita: Per unit of the population.

satellite: Something that branches off from or revolves around a central body.

toxoplasmosis: An illness caused by a parasite that can be acquired from eating undercooked meat, contact with cat feces, or eating unpasteurized dairy products. This illness is usually mild in adults, but can cause grave illness in babies.

vocalized: Made noises with the vocal chords.

INDEX

BIOGRAPHIES

Autumn Libal is a graduate of Smith College and works as a freelance writer and illustrator in Northeastern Pennsylvania. She has written for other Mason Crest series, including NORTH AMERICAN FOLKLORE, NORTH AMERICAN INDIANS TODAY, and PSYCHIATRIC DISORDERS: DRUGS AND PSYCHOLOGY FOR THE MIND AND BODY.

Dr. Lisa Albers is a developmental behavioral pediatrician at Children's Hospital Boston and Harvard Medical School, where her responsibilities include outpatient pediatric teaching and patient care in the Developmental Medicine Center. She currently is Director of the Adoption Program, Director of Fellowships in Developmental and Behavioral Pediatrics, and collaborates in a consultation program for community health centers. She is also the school consultant for the Walker School, a residential school for children in the state foster care system.

Dr. Carolyn Bridgemohan is an instructor in pediatrics at Harvard Medical School and is a board-certified developmental behavioral pediatrician on staff in the Developmental Medicine Center at Children's Hospital, Boston. Her clinical practice includes children and youth with autism, hearing impairment, developmental language disorders, global delays, mental retardation, and attention and learning disorders. Dr. Bridgemohan is coeditor of *Bright Futures Case Studies for Primary Care Clinicians: Child Development and Behavior*, a curriculum used nationwide in pediatric residency training programs.

Cindy Croft is the State Special Needs Director in Minnesota, coordinating Project EXCEPTIONAL MN, through Concordia University. Project EXCEPTIONAL MN is a state project that supports the inclusion of children in community settings through training, on-site consultation, and professional development. She also teaches as adjunct faculty for Concordia University, St. Paul, Minnesota. She has worked in the special needs arena for the past fifteen years.

Dr. Laurie Glader is a developmental pediatrician at Children's Hospital in Boston where she directs the Cerebral Palsy Program and is a staff pediatrician with the Coordinated Care Services, a program designed to meet the needs of children with special health care needs. Dr. Glader also teaches regularly at Harvard Medical School. Her work with public agencies includes New England SERVE, an organization that builds connections between state health departments, health care organizations, community providers, and families. She is also the staff physician at the Cotting School, a school specializing in the education of children with a wide range of special health care needs.

DATE DUE

JAN 2 9 2008			
APR 1 3 2009			